PROOF OF THE PUDDING

PHOEBE ATWOOD TAYLOR

PROOF
OF THE
PUDDING

An Asey Mayo Cape Cod Mystery

A Foul Play Press Book

THE COUNTRYMAN PRESS
Woodstock, Vermont

Copyright © 1945 by Phoebe Atwood Taylor

This edition published in 1991 by Foul Play Press, an imprint
of The Countryman Press, Inc., Woodstock, Vermont 05091.

ISBN 0-88150-193-X

Printed in the United States of America

For A.M.F.

ONE

Asey Mayo slid the steamer trunk over the side of the red jeep, watched it thud down among the dry leaves beside his two kitbags, and then once again looked expectantly across the yard toward his house.

"I wonder what's keeping her," he murmured curiously to himself.

His housekeeper cousin Jennie Mayo certainly must be at home. The doors and windows were open, and spirals of smoke curled above the chimneys into the bright blue October sky. Furthermore, a spicy odor of sugar gingerbread and apple turnovers and plum cake issued from the kitchen ell, suggesting that in some psychic way, Jennie must even have guessed he was coming back to Cape Cod, and was baking in a big way for his return.

Probably, Asey decided as he picked up his trench coat and brief case and jumped lightly to the ground, probably she was so busy killing fatted calves for the Prodigal, she hadn't heard him drive into the yard or blow the horn.

He was carrying his bags up the oystershell walk to the back door when screams of uncontrollable laughter, bursting suddenly out of the pine grove beyond the house, stopped him in his tracks.

Someone began to beat loudly on a tin pan. Women's voices rose in song. A little raggedly at first, and then with lusty enthusiasm, the unseen choir rolled out the barrel, because the gang was all there. At the end of the chorus, the effort petered away and dissolved into more shrieks of laughter, only to pick up again with renewed spirit and an overtone of harmony. After a couple of false starts, the tin pan beater finally caught the rhythm.

Grinning broadly, Asey leaned against the short white picket fence, and looked down toward the boathouse in the direction of the noise.

Apparently Jennie had not only found out that he was heading home, but she had somehow even managed to diagnose the exact moment of his arrival.

"An' so," he said with a chuckle, "she's gone an' planned an ovation for me!"

After four years of seeing him only at rare intervals, Jennie probably had an ovation stored up in her system, he decided, and he might as well face the music and get it over with. Somewhat self-consciously, he straightened his tie, buttoned his coat, and waited.

"For Pete's sakes!" Asey felt his jaw drop at his first sight of the procession which finally emerged up the narrow path through the scrub pines. "For *Pete's* sakes!"

Jennie, smudged and aproned and dust-capped, stalwartly gripping a sawhorse under either arm, bustled along at the head of the group. The rest of the dozen-odd women, similarly dressed in somewhat grubby workaday attire, were more conservative in their choice of burdens, and merely carried long planks and wooden kegs between them. A small plump girl in dungarees and a tentlike white sweater provided the tin pan obbligato.

As the scarlet jeep came into the line of vision of the first few pairs, they stopped unevenly, causing audible objections and some barked-knuckle casualties among the rear rank of plank toters who couldn't yet see what lay ahead.

"A jeep, a jeep! A *red* jeep!" The plump little girl sounded like a sparrow. "Look, Jennie, a *jeep!*"

But Jennie ignored her chirpings. Her gaze had already jumped beyond the vehicle in the yard and the luggage sitting beside it. With her mouth wide open in amazement, she was staring at her cousin.

"Hi!" Asey said cheerfully. "How are you?"

"Hi." Jennie set the sawhorses down very slowly. "Hi."

During the uncomfortable little moment of silence that ensued, three things dawned on Asey in rapid succession.

This was no planned ovation—he had simply interrupted some strange impromptu robbing of his boathouse fixtures. No one, including Jennie herself, had any remote inkling of the possibility of his return. And to judge from the stark anguish written on the faces of the group, his arrival at this time was nothing short of a major calamity.

In a nutshell, he was no Prodigal. He was a Problem, an unforeseen contingency, a monkey wrench in whatever works were going on.

"Hi," Jennie said again, and forced the corners of her mouth to arch themselves into a brightly artificial smile. "Well, well, this certainly is a sur*prise,* all right! Isn't this a—uh—a pleasant surprise, girls?"

The girls, who didn't have Jennie's ability to pick up quickly, managed to nod agreement, but they still looked pretty glum to Asey. Their morale visibly soared, however, when Jennie turned and whispered something to them.

"Well, well!" Jennie marched over to him with her hand outstretched. "I guess from the looks of all your baggage, you're home for good! Did the Porter Plant get reconverted?"

"Uh-huh, we got the news yesterday. So I started—"

"Well, well! If you'd only given me some warnin', I'd have had things *ready* for you! But your boats are ready, anyway—and you know what I bet?"

Her warmly jovial tones as she took his arm and started to steer him toward the back door caused Asey to look at her sharply and with something akin to suspicion. Jennie never laid it on with a trowel like that unless she had some ulterior motives.

"I bet," she continued with the same exaggerated heartiness, "that you can't *wait* to get into your old clothes! You're *yearnin'* to get out fishin', aren't you? Well, your corduroys an' flannel shirt an' all are hangin' right up in your closet." She gave him a little push. "Get along—I'll fix you up a nice lunch to take, an' you can start right off, in ten minutes. Five, if you hustle!"

Asey disengaged his arm. "But I'm not in any rush to go fishin'," he said. "I got all the time in the world. Besides, I been drivin' all night," he nodded toward the jeep, "in Junior."

Jennie wasted only the most casual glance on the vehicle. "Where'd you get that contraption? Whatever are you goin' to *do* with it?"

Asey looked at her quizzically. Ever since the first jeep had appeared in the public eye, Jennie had coveted one for her very own. To the best of his knowledge and belief, a jeep had been her postwar dream child.

"I got Junior at an army salvage sale," he said. "The boys at the Porter Plant fixed it up—"

Before he could add, "as a present for you," she interrupted him.

"Asey, I tell you what. If you don't feel like goin' out fishin' now, then I guess you better rush right over an' hunt up those blinds over in the inlet woods."

"Did you say *blinds?*" Asey sounded as confused as he felt. "In the inlet woods? *Blinds?*"

"Blinds! *Our* blinds! Are *you* blind?" Jennie demanded with some asperity. "Haven't you noticed all our missin' blinds? Oh, Asey Mayo, don't you know we just had a hurricane? Why, I wrote you, an' sent clippin's, an' pictures—didn't you bother to read about it? Didn't you *see* the damage with your own two eyes this mornin'? Why, a blind man couldn't miss all them uprooted trees, an' all the smashed-up houses!"

"I wasn't as interested in lookin' at the scenery as I was in keepin' Junior on the road," Asey returned. "We had a good twenty miles of fresh unsanded oil to cope with on the home stretch, an' Junior's sort of skittish—ooop, sorry!" He flattened himself against the picket fence as two of the women, lugging Jennie's discarded sawhorses, all but crowded him off the walk. "Don't look at me so indignant, Jennie. Sure I knew you'd had a blow!"

"Call our *hurr*icane a blow, do you? Well, Mister Codfish Sherlock, you'd better start right in findin' out what the *blow* did to our town, an'—oh, *do* look out! You're in the way of that board!"

Asey ducked the end of the wide pine plank which two

more women were clumsily engineering through the back door.

"Yes, sir," Jennie went on, "just you do a little of your old sleuthin' around Pogue inlet shore, an' locate those blinds before someone else walks off with 'em. I guess before you're through, you'll learn what kind of a *blow* we had! Oh, dear, you're awful in the *way,* standin' here! Pick up your bags an' go in*side*—no, no! You can't stay in the kitchen, Asey! There's not a single *speck* of room there!"

She forcibly propelled him through the kitchen ell and on into the dining room before he had more than a fleeting glimpse of what seemed to be two million pies and three million cakes.

"Now," Jennie gave him no chance to ask any questions as she swung open the door at the foot of the back stairs, "you go right up an' change, an' get started after those blinds!"

"You can't be," Asey said gently.

"I can't be what?"

"Serious. Honest, you don't expect me to go wanderin' off a mile across the inlet to hunt for blinds that blew off—how long ago? Nearly three weeks?"

"Pogue inlet's where they were headin' when *I* last saw 'em!" Jennie retorted. "Most of the blinds from this section flew over there."

"So?" Ignoring the door which she was still holding open, Asey sauntered over and sat down in an armchair before the dining-room fireplace.

"Yes, that's *so!* Trouble is, you don't understand what's happened! Why, not more'n half the phones are back in service yet, an' we only got electricity the day before yesterday. Nobody's been let go near that part of the beach till today, an' I'd have gone myself this mornin' if I hadn't been so busy—no, no, Mattie! Not there! Wait, an' I'll *show* you! Tch, tch, tch!" Clucking her tongue indignantly, Jennie bounced out to the kitchen.

Asey leaned back in the armchair and thoughtfully pulled out his pipe and filled it. While Jennie had maneuvered him into any number of odd, wild-goose chores in years gone by, it occurred to him that he'd never before seen her quite so blatantly anxious to get him out of the way.

He wondered why, as he looked around. The dining room, the living room beyond, and the segment of front parlor visible to him all seemed even spicker and spanner than usual. The furniture was waxed within an inch of its life, the slip covers were freshly laundered, the ruffled curtains were stiff with starch, and the windowpanes practically glared in the sun. It was company glow, all right.

"You mind moving, please?"

Asey glanced up at the trio standing beside him. "No, certainly not. Need my chair?"

"Thanks." They whisked it off into the parlor.

"You can't stand *there*, Asey!" Jennie informed him when she returned from the kitchen. "That's where I want the whatnot put, Ellen. Exactly right where he's standin'—*please* get out of the way, will you, Asey?"

"Yes, ma'am." He sat down on a sawhorse which was snatched from under him almost at once. "I think I'm gettin' the idea, Jennie. Sawhorses an' planks make tables, an' all that food means a cake sale. Now *why* in the world are you tryin' to drive me away from a simple cake sale?"

"It's not," Jennie said. "It's more of a lawn fête, an' I'm sure you're perfectly welcome to stay. *If* you think you'll enjoy it an' *not* feel you're in the *way*—an' if you don't get those great kitbags out from underfoot, someone's goin' to trip an' break their necks. Put them on the stairs, for goodness' sakes!"

Asey removed the offending bags, and then returned to watch the improvised tables receive their camouflage in the shape of fresh white tablecloths.

"*Mind* that vase of chrysanthemums Mary's carryin'!" Jennie said. "Really, I *do* think you could find a better place to lean against than that door, with everyone passin' by! Perhaps you better sit on the stairs until the flowers get fixed!"

Five minutes later, she tartly pointed out to him that people were having to detour around his feet, and that it might on the whole prove beneficial if he were to edge up the stairs a bit. When the plates of food were brought in from the kitchen, a sharp protest followed his casual gesture of reaching out and helping himself to an apple turnover.

"That'll be ten cents, an' don't you spill one crumb on—what're you murmurin' about under your breath?"

"Fatted calves," Asey told her.

"*Whose?*" Jennie demanded with rising inflection, and a sideways glance at the other women. "*Whose* fatted calves, I'd like to know?"

"A certain man's," Asey said. "Anonymous, with two sons. An' I bet I never succumb to any more prodigal illusions! Here's a dollar—give me that plate of turnovers before I succumb to starvation, too. An' d'you think," he lowered his voice to a whisper, "maybe I'd better take 'em up to my room an' eat 'em there?"

Jennie chose to take his irony seriously. "I certainly think it'd *look* better—get along!" She followed him up the stairs. "Asey, I knew you wouldn't much like my havin' this to-do here," she went on a little penitently, "an' I'm sorry it happened the day you came back. But I *had* to have it. You see, *I* got to raise more rebuildin' money than anyone else—*drat* that old hurricane! It was all my fault, really!"

"The hurricane?"

"No, no, of course not! I mean the in*surance—please* watch those crumbs! You know after the thirty-eight hurricane, everyone said there'd never be another in a hundred years? You said so, yourself! Well, *I* thought, why waste money? So I went an' took the hurricane insurance off the Women's Club clubhouse."

"Oh-oh! An' did it get hurt?" Asey asked.

"Hurt?" Jennie sniffed. "All we got left to start in with is the millstone we used for a front doorstep. An' Roberts' Rules of Order. I found that under a forsythia bush down the lane. So that's why I'm havin' this business here this after—"

She broke off at the sound of someone scrambling up the steep stairs behind them.

The plump little girl in the dungarees and the baggy white sweater was so out of breath on the top step that she choked, and had to be patted on the back.

"This's Mildred. Mildred Rayson," Jennie said parenthetically to Asey. "I guess you wouldn't remember her. She was just a little snippet when you saw her last. There, I guess you're all right now —did you want something?"

"Maybe," Asey suggested blandly, "it's got to be *her* turn."

"Her turn for what?"

"To tell me to edge a little farther out of the way, please," Asey returned.

Jennie ignored his gibe. "What is it, Mildred?"

"Mother thought—I mean," Mildred said breathlessly, "*I* thought that *he*—that Mr. Mayo—would maybe want to buy some of my cards, perhaps."

"Sure he will—Mildred's helpin' to raise money, too," Jennie explained. "She's sellin' packets of hurricane postcards that her big brother prints up. Give her a quarter, Asey. If you didn't bother readin' the clippin's I sent you, those cards'll show you what we looked like day after the *blow!*"

"Thank you very much." Mildred thrust the cards into Asey's hand. "Oh, and mother says to tell you the Skaket crowd's come, Jennie. Already."

"No! Never! So *soon?* So—" Jennie paused and looked at Asey.

"Don't fret, cousin," he said. "If you're so dead set on gettin' me out of the way, I'll sneak into my room an' hide there."

"That's just it, you *can't!* You see, we're havin' a little play, too, an' that group's usin' *my* room for a dressin' room. An' then there's goin' to be music by the Women's Club quartet an' orchestra, in costume, an' *they're* usin' *your* room to dress in. So you can't stay *here* now— Asey Mayo, what're you doin'?"

"Openin' the window," Asey said. "You were mighty smart to hold out that little play an' the music for your trump card, knowin' my reactions to 'em both. I know when I'm licked, Jennie. I'm goin' to take my boughten fatted calves an' go hunt blinds until this clambake an' jive session's finished!"

To Mildred's squealing delight and Jennie's unfeigned horror, he ducked out through the window, reached back inside for his plate of turnovers, and walked off along the flat roof of the kitchen ell.

"So long!"

Still holding in one hand the plate of apple turnovers, he swung down to the roof of the woodshed, slid down from there to the chopping-block stump, and from that he stepped to the ground.

A moment later, the red jeep was bounding out of the yard.

While Jennie's conspiracy to edge him out of the way had amused him, Asey found himself wondering as he drove off just what her motive was. Ordinarily, she enjoyed nothing more than showing him off in his city clothes, and particularly to her Women's Club friends. It couldn't be any idle whim that forced her to such efforts to get rid of him, he decided. She must have felt it to be a matter of vital importance.

He'd find out the real reason some time, he supposed. Some time when she got good and ready to tell him. In the meantime, he intended to locate his friend Dr. Cummings, and sandwich in a chat between the doctor's calls.

Never for one moment had it occurred to him to take seriously Jennie's orders to hunt up the blown-off blinds. But his first close-up view of Pogue inlet snatched his attention away from the road so completely that Junior started to swerve into the ditch.

Asey jerked the car back on the road, switched off the motor, and stared unbelievingly at the debris-strewn beach.

Then he got out.

Fifteen minutes later, he was still sitting on the shore, staring.

He was now entirely willing to admit that there was no reason why his blinds shouldn't be here. Practically everything else was.

Out of the rubble beyond the water line he had identified such widely diverse items as a hunk of Spooner's red barn, which had stood a mile north of his house, and an arm of Ed Savory's wind-mill, originally some two miles to the south. Pieces of lobster pots and smashed boats rubbed elbows with parts of rocking chairs and tables and sofas. A garden hose reel stood proudly by a rock. Draped against one of its wheels was the sideboard of a blue farm wagon.

From where he sat, he could now see what was left of the sum-mer colony over at the neck. It actually looked, he thought a little wryly, like the pictures painted of it a few years back by a class of long-haired surrealists. There were a lot of drunken walls sur-rounding nothing at all, a few odd chimneys and bathtubs and latticed porches quite unattached to anything else, and five brand new, bulbous sand dunes. The old Neck Inn alone could lay any claim to being intact. Its upper floors were fine and whole. But they were perched precariously on four toothpicklike uprights, and the incoming tide was splashing gently through what had once been the main lobby.

Asey shook his head at the changes wrought in the harbor. And the silhouette of the town proper puzzled him for some time before he began to grasp what was wrong. It was the trees. Or, rather, the lack of them. For the towering elms had disappeared from the center. The steeple had gone from the Congregational Church, too, and the town hall was shy its memorial clock tower.

The longer he sat and looked, the more sensible it seemed to postpone his contemplated call on Cummings, and to hunt up those missing blinds instead.

He wouldn't be the only scavenger in the vicinity. Three boys were trying to salvage a half-sunken sharpie jammed into the breakwater, a couple of men were dragging for their lost lobster pots in the shallow water offshore, some girls were excitedly pok-ing around the flotsam. Farther along, up by the town landing, a group struggled to remove what seemed to be a garage door from the roof of a boathouse. Beyond him, up among the pines, a woman was walking in a beeline, her head bent down and her eyes fixed on the ground. Whatever she was hunting, she was going at the process determinedly and according to Hoyle. After pacing off ten yards, she would move over perhaps two inches, and pace ten yards back, then move over another two inches and begin again. Obviously, Asey thought as he got to his feet, she was searching for something smaller than blinds.

Picking up the empty turnover plate, he considered the problem of where to begin.

He smiled as he recalled the lost-horse maxim of Jennie's husband Syl, which the latter applied with amazing success to the retrieving of all lost, strayed, or misplaced items.

"I just figger it out," Syl would drawl, "if I was a hoss, why where would I go to? N'en I go there, an' it most usually is."

Asey shifted the plate to his left hand.

"Now, let's figger," he murmured. "If I was our blinds, where'd I have flown to? Huh. That stuff along the shore washed in with the tide. Anything blown right here on the beach would've been smashed into matchwood weeks ago. Anything still here an' still whole would have to have landed back farther in the woods, I'd say—oh, for the love of Pete, I can't set off on a blind-hunt luggin' this fool thing!"

He attempted, as he started off through the bushes, to stuff the plate into his coat pocket, and ended up by still carrying it in his hand.

If only Dr. Cummings would conveniently ask him what he'd been doing, Asey thought! But the doctor wouldn't believe him. No one would ever believe his honest report that he'd been hunting his upstairs blinds over in Pogue inlet woods, wearing the while his best city clothes, and lugging in his hand an empty plate decorated with hand-painted rosebuds!

"Stop there!"

The command, called out with such sharp authority, caused Asey to swing around in surprise. He hadn't heard anyone moving about near him.

He found a tall, hatless man in gray tweeds standing by a clump of scrub oaks, and eyeing him with evident and marked disapproval.

"Hullo," Asey said. "Quite a sight along the inlet, isn't it? I hadn't seen it bef—"

"D'you have some identification?"

The question itself, rather than the way it was shot at him, amazed Asey so that he blinked. After all, this was his own bailiwick, where everyone knew him at least by sight, or recognized him from rotogravure pictures!

Then he reminded himself that he was wearing city clothes, and not the corduroys and duck coat and yachting cap which Jennie wiltingly referred to as his Codfish Sherlock or Hayseed Sleuth outfit.

"Guess I can accommodate you." Asey started to reach for his wallet, and remembered that he'd left it on the dining-room table when he took out his tobacco pouch. "Huh, guess I can't, at that. But my name's Mayo, an' I'm reasonably well known hereabouts. Uh—any particular reason for wantin' to identify me?"

The man raised his heavy blackthorn walking stick and pointed the end of it accusingly toward the plate in Asey's hand.

"When we see strangers with household goods," he said crisply, "we've learned to make inquiries. Is that your plate?"

"Yes." But on looking at it closely, Asey suddenly realized that it wasn't one of Jennie's, after all. "Uh—no. No, it's not. I guess maybe you might say that I bought it."

"Indeed! May I suggest to you that if you *buy*," the man paused significantly, "if you *buy* anything else, you take the precaution of securing a bill of sale? Remember that!"

"May I ask," Asey began, "who you—"

But the man had turned on his heel and was striding away with righteous indignation practically rising in a halo above his iron-gray hair.

Asey grinned. "What a home comin'! First I'm a monkey wrench, now I'm a looter! Wa-el, I suppose he meant all right!"

Strolling along through the pines, he all but stumbled upon a jagged piece of roof which he at once recognized from the color of the splintered shingles.

"If that hunk of Higgins's green mansard roof sailed all the way over here," he said to himself, "I guess my blinds aren't far off— now what do you know about that? Cod line!"

He leaned over, picked up the dangling end of line from the bayberry bushes among which Higgins' roof reposed, and examined it with a critical eye.

It was new, unused, and certainly better than any which he possessed.

"Maybe it's lootin', but no thrifty Mayo could pass up a good piece of cod line!" he said, and promptly proceeded to wind it around the turnover plate.

As he walked along, still winding, he wondered how such a length of line could have become unwound in such an odd fashion. Certainly it couldn't have been blown into this mathematically straight line by any hurricane. Not even by a hurricane that had planted the Women's Club's Rules of Order under a forsythia bush!

If only the end which he'd picked up had been hitched to anything, like a reel or a stick, he would guess that someone had been trying to mark off a land boundary. But it hadn't even been hooked over one of the jags of that conveniently located hunk of mansard roof. It was just dangling, just loose.

After the beach scenes, Asey felt he should be willing to accept almost any bizarre state of affairs as a logical and normal result of the storm. But the longer he continued to reel in cod line around the turnover plate, the more thoroughly curious he became.

No Cape Codder in his right mind would ever stretch a couple of hundred feet of new cod line on the ground with such precise care, and then go away and forget it!

Nor would anyone else, when you came right down to brass tacks. Jennie, of course, would merely cluck her tongue at the situation and make disparaging cracks about the peculiarities of summer folks. But this was the first week of October, past the time for summer folks to be around. Summer folks, moreover, didn't ordinarily go in for this kind of deep-sea line, or for so much of it.

While he paused to rest his wrist, which was getting tired from winding, he noticed that there was a path cut through the woods ahead of him. Probably the cod line would stop there, he decided. After all, it had to stop somewhere!

An experimental jerk, as he began reeling in again, showed no indication of any slackness in the offing. It didn't feel as if he were coming to the end.

"Who knows," he murmured, "who knows? Maybe this is the start of a project to prove one of those sentences, like 'If-you-wound-a-string-around-the-earth, then-you'd-find-such-and-such-true.' But why start in the Pogue inlet woods, of *all* places?"

Still winding, he started across the path, only to stop so abruptly that he had to grab at a pine branch to keep from falling headlong.

Directly in front of him, face down on the path, with the cod line passing over her shoulders, lay a girl.

She was dead.

Asey sensed that even before he knelt down beside her.

Furthermore, he thought grimly, she couldn't very well have died, and then put that cod line over herself!

TWO

WHEN he got to his feet a few moments later, Asey asked himself if this perhaps was the solution of the cod-line puzzle, if it had been deliberately stretched out to guide or lead or entice someone to this scene?

But he dismissed the thought almost as soon as it occurred to him.

After all, no one had any reason to waste time on such an involved and laborious and futile gesture. This was a well-used path, and any passer-by couldn't fail to find the girl. There was no need to plant a dangling end of cod line among bayberry bushes in the hope that some wandering, eagle-eyed scavenger, while gaping at the piece of mansard roof, might possibly spot the line and follow it here.

Once again Asey bent down and looked thoughtfully at the girl. It occurred to him that he was letting his own personal curiosity about that infernal line overshadow the problem of her identity, which should have been his first concern.

"Curly brown hair, medium height, slim, in her early twenties." That was what he would shortly be telling the police over the telephone.

"Her hair's got a streak of white about an inch wide in front. Maybe painted on, I wouldn't know. No, *I* don't know who she is. No idea."

He wouldn't trouble to qualify that by adding his impression that the girl's face was very vaguely familiar, as if he had known someone who looked like her. She even might be someone he actually had known but who, like the overweight little Mildred, had grown up and changed her contours during the last few years.

"No, I don't know *who* killed her." The cops would be sure to ask that one, Asey thought. They always did. "No, she wasn't shot, or stabbed—at least as far as I can tell. Poisoned? Nuh-uh, I don't think so! No, I *don't* think she just died, either. I think she met with what you boys call foul play. Because—look, it's like this From her position, it *seems* as if she'd plunged forward, as if she'd been tripped while runnin'. Only I somehow don't think she was. An' then there's this cod line—cod line. Fish line. That's it. Cod line. Was she strangled? No, that's one thing I'm certain of. No— listen! This cod line, see, is *over* her—"

He sighed. There he was, stumped by that cod line again!

There was no question about it, he really ought to solve that cod-line angle before he came in any contact with the cops. He couldn't, for example, visualize himself trying to explain to his old friend, Lieutenant Hanson, just how he happened to be winding cod line on a turnover plate with rosebuds, while hunting blinds in the woods! Certainly he couldn't do that over the phone. Even in person, it would be a long, hard pull.

"Okay, then!" he said aloud. "Figure it out! Did she fall, or was she tripped? Or what? An' what *about* that line?"

A brief but careful survey of the path showed absolutely nothing over which she could have stumbled. The toes of her brown alligator pumps hadn't been stubbed, the high heels hadn't been wrenched or twisted, the leather heel lifts gave no evidence of having been caught on or in anything.

Could the line have been rigged up in such a way that it might have tripped her?

Asey doubted it. That line was too long to have been drawn taut enough to offer sufficient resistance. And had she tripped in the slack, the line should now be tangled around her feet or her ankles, and not draped carefully over the raglan shoulders of her brown gabardine coat.

Of course it was the brown coat, blending so perfectly with the sere oak leaves and dried pine needles, which had kept him from seeing her until he was almost on top of her. But that fact wouldn't interest the police any. And they would notice as quickly as he had the contrast between her and, say, the women in wash dresses or slacks and sweaters who'd been milling around his house. The latter, even when they'd changed into their best for the lawn fête, could never manage to look like this girl. The diamond and topaz flower in her lapel probably cost more than the accumulated wardrobes of the whole Women's Club for a year. Her tiny, diamond-studded wrist watch would unquestionably have rebuilt the demolished clubhouse several times over.

In passing, Asey noted that the watch was still running, and that it was within a few minutes of three o'clock, which checked with his own watch. That would please Dr. Cummings, who habitually wrote fiery letters of protest to authors of detective stories in which the time of the murder was accurately placed by the time indicated on the stopped wrist watch of the deceased.

Her coat label indicated that she patronized the same exclusive shop in New York where his boss's wife, Betsey Porter, ran up such awe-inspiring bills. The chamois gloves in her pocket were handmade. The handkerchief stuffed in with them was fine, sheer linen.

"What's the matter with me?" Asey asked himself irritably. "I'm asleep! If she's this dressed up, of course she had a pocketbook!"

His brisk search on either side of the path unearthed a brown alligator envelope, nearly as large as his own brief case. For all its size, its contents were distinctly disappointing. Instead of the usual feminine conglomeration of miscellaneous items, this merely contained money—two hundred dollars in crisp new ten dollar bills. As if, Asey thought, she'd casually cashed a check, and said in response to the teller's inevitable question, "Oh, anything—yes, tens. Tens will do."

There was nothing bearing her name, or even her initials. But the cops wouldn't have any trouble finding out who she was. There was nothing nondescript about her, from her topaz pin to the white streak in her hair.

He looked again at the cod line, idly touched it, and shook his head.

Perhaps it would be just as well not to mention it at all to the cops. Let Hanson and his boys get themselves all wound up in knots doping it out. He'd just report having found the girl, suggest that in his opinion it was a job for them, and they could take it and carry on from there.

Better still, he decided as he put the pocketbook down beside her and stood up again, he wouldn't even phone the cops himself. He'd go back to the shore, ask one of the lobstermen or debris hunters to call Dr. Cummings, who was the medical examiner, and ask him to call Hanson. Before the latter or any of his men arrived, Cummings would have reached the scene, and have contributed his opinion of the situation. Or, rather, his opinions. Cummings was not one to confine himself to one paltry opinion.

Asey suspected that the cod line would probably baffle Cummings, too. But he'd be very much surprised if the doctor didn't at once question the lack of evidence of her falling or tripping, as well as the lack of marks or bruises on her face, considering that she had apparently fallen on it with such headlong force.

He was also sure that the doctor would feel that there was something phony about the girl's position, and agree with him that she actually hadn't fallen that way, but that she had been placed that way.

And Cummings would certainly raise his eyebrows when he was shown how far the pocketbook had been from her. If she'd been holding it properly, that underarm bag should have fallen very near her—indeed, the chances were that she might never have let go of it at all. Even if she'd been carrying a corner of the bag in her hand, no fall or tripping could ever have jolted it into flying to the spot where he'd found it. Someone, Asey thought, had slipped up very badly on that pocketbook planting. They hadn't figured it out enough.

Yes, long before Hanson turned up, Cummings would know exactly where she had been hit, if not exactly what had hit her, or who.

Because someone surely had!

And it hadn't been anything less than a masterly bash, a quick one to the right spot. Cummings would unquestionably deliver a monologue of professional praise for the skill of such an expert basher.

"I wonder, now," Asey murmured, "if I was some innocent passer-by, just how much I'd have questioned her position! Probably I'd have been too shocked at findin' her to question much. I wonder how much I'd have moved her around, tryin' to make sure if she wasn't maybe alive. Because it looked like she fell or tripped, I think I'd take it for granted that she fell or tripped. I don't think the possibility of a bash would ever enter my head!"

In fact, if he hadn't actually already been curious about the cod line, and in an inquiring frame of mind, would he have been quite so suspicious, himself?

It was probably a very good thing that he had been, but he must curb his suspicions and watch out that they didn't run away with him. Particularly in the matter of that tall man with the blackthorn stick. He mustn't let that fellow enter his mind. True, he had been wandering around the pines. True, he had an excellent instrument for bashing right in his hand.

"But the good lord only knows how many other handy blunt instruments there are scattered about this vicinity," he said, "from Higgins's mansard roof to that arm of Savory's windmill. An' the garden hose reel. An' if the shore was so full of people, the woods could've been full, too. Nope, Mayo, put that man out of your mind! Put the cod line out of your mind! Get along, an' get someone to phone to Cummings!"

As he started to turn back to the beach, something stirred in the leaves by his feet.

A snake?

He looked down, and gave an experimental little stamp with his foot.

Then he realized that the leaves were stirring because the rosebud plate, over which he'd wound the cod line, and which he'd set down on the ground, was moving!

He blinked.

It couldn't be moving! He'd simply done so much staring and peering and viewing and looking, with his eyes already tired from that long drive in Junior, that he was seeing things!

But the leaves stirred again as the plate gave a little bounce upward.

It wasn't any mirage.

That plate actually was moving!

Asey bit back the exclamation that jumped to his lips.

Of course it was moving!

Of course—and why not? Someone was reeling in the other end of the cod line!

He wanted suddenly to shout out at the top of his lungs that he was a silly fool, the biggest goon in a dozen counties! Here a perfectly obvious solution to the cod-line puzzle had been staring him in the face, and like Columbus and the egg, someone had to show him how it worked before he had the wit to figure it out!

Of course the line hadn't been laid down to entice someone like himself *to* the girl, but to guide someone else *back* to her!

Noiselessly, he ducked behind the thickest of the pines, and crouched down low in the bayberry bushes at the foot of the trunk.

It all began to make some sense, now, he told himself.

He recalled that the path on which the girl lay was clearly exposed to view from the shore in at least a dozen places. If someone wished to avoid being seen, that path was definitely a very bad bet. Someone, consequently, had left the cod line stretched out at right angles to the path so that it could act as a guide back to the girl's body, either from the shore side where he himself had found it, or from the other end, from which this someone was now cautiously reeling in.

Of course, he mentally amended, anyone coming up as he had from the beach ran plenty of chances of being seen. But under the circumstances, with all the hurricane aftermath, someone pretending to be a flotsam hunter could stroll casually up into the woods without attracting any particular attention. Someone sneaking along the path, on the other hand, would run far more danger of being noticed, and remembered later.

From where he was crouching, he could see the rosebud plate give another little hop up into the air. Something about the movement reminded him of corn just beginning to pop in a hot skillet.

Then the plate began to bounce furiously, as the unseen reeler apparently indulged in a violent burst of rapid winding.

A few inches at a time, it jumped across the pine needles and onto the path itself.

Asey held his breath.

He had originally put the plate down on his side of the path, on a spot slightly above the girl's outstretched hands.

Was it now going to be dragged down diagonally, and become caught on them?

Certainly the reeler would then know, if he hadn't already guessed, that something was on the end of his line, that it wasn't any longer just loosely dangling!

Why hadn't the fellow become suspicious, anyway? Or had he simply assumed that his line must have caught on some small object in its passage back, and was just temporarily dragging it along?

The plate gave a sudden jump past the girl's fingertips, just grazing them, and then hopped across to the far side of the path.

Asey let himself breathe again.

Now the plate's course over the carpet of pine needles was reasonably clear and safe for a matter of fifteen or twenty feet. At the speed the line was now being reeled in, the reeler himself shouldn't be frightened away by any snags until he caught up with the plate.

But a perverse bounce caused the line to coil over the end of a good-sized twig.

And the twig, sliding sideways, caught among the branches of a tiny pine seedling.

And stayed there.

The frantic jiggles of the line, as the reeler tried to jerk hard enough to force the plate to move on, were almost hypnotically fascinating to watch. But each successive jerk merely settled the twig and the line and the plate a little more firmly among the small flexible branches, which bent parallel to the ground but wouldn't give way.

Asey asked himself how much longer it would take for the lubber to sense the finality of the line snag and depart rapidly somewhere else.

As if in answer to his question, the line immediately slackened. Now what, Asey wondered. Now what?

Obviously the fellow would either have to leave his line there, or else walk up to where it was caught, and untangle it.

"But if it was me," Asey thought, "I'd be inclined to do some reconnoiterin' first, in any case. Huh. I guess I'll just stay put, an' wait, an' see!"

Still crouched down, he waited, and peered, and listened.

Five minutes passed.

Then another five.

His eyes felt strained from trying to pick out some moving object among the pines, and his ears ached from listening for some tell-tale rustlings, or for the cautious pad of footsteps.

Colonies of ants were feasting hungrily on his right ankle, two wasps were using his forehead as a landing strip, and he was choking back an almost overwhelming impulse to sneeze.

But what made him most uncomfortable was the belated realization that he might just possibly have crowed too soon in assuming that he'd got the solution of the cod-line puzzle.

Sober second thought wasn't pinning any medals on his first excited guess.

For if the person had been using the line as a guide back to the girl's body, as he'd figured, then why had he stood off at a distance and reeled the line in, instead of walking back to her?

In short, the line might well not have been a guide, at all.

"An'," Asey muttered as he got to his feet, "I've had enough of it, whatever it is!"

He stretched his cramped shoulders, leaned down and scratched vigorously at his ankle, and concluded that whatever this little episode may have signified, he certainly hadn't won.

He knew no more about the line than he had in the first place; he hadn't seen the reeler-inner and he probably never would. If the fellow hadn't departed forever, he was most likely sitting in some comfortable, sequestered, antless spot, cheerfully waiting until he had the woods to himself.

And what he might then propose to do with his confounded cod line was his own sweet business, and Asey refused to let his mind dwell on it another minute. No more fruitless brooding over that line. He was through.

"An' if Hanson an' Cummings ask me what *I* think," he said, "I'll tell 'em—*I* think he's an old string saver, an' every October he comes out from under his mossy rock, an' hunts cod li—"

The sound of a branch breaking, over in the woods to his left, came with all the surprise shock of a summer thunderclap.

It wasn't an underfoot sound of someone stepping on something, but a definite crack, as if someone had reached up and snapped off a dead branch.

Asey hesitated.

Probably it was better to catch a glimpse of anyone in the vicinity, even an innocent fellow blind-hunter, than to stand like a stump, figuring and brooding and calculating, and getting exactly nowhere.

But he kept wishing, as he quietly started toward the sound, that he was twins. He didn't really want to leave either the girl or the line alone. There'd been almost a touch of a come-on element in the distinctness of that noise, following so long and so solid a silence. It was almost as if someone had derisively yelled out, "Yoo-hoo, here I am!"

Another branch cracked, still farther to his left.

Slowly, still hesitant, Asey turned in the direction of the new sound.

A moment later, beyond his sight but almost dead ahead of him, someone started to run.

Asey went after him.

His sense of relief at finally having something tangible to chase was so intense that he wouldn't particularly have cared whether he was sprinting over pine needles or red-hot coals.

Plunging and ducking through bushes, twisting and skidding around trees, sliding on the slippery needles, he raced along, following the sound of the fleet footsteps ahead.

He was gaining. He was sure of it. But he still wasn't near enough to catch a glimpse of the man.

Pausing for a split second to listen and check on his direction, Asey was dumbfounded to hear another set of footsteps.

Behind him.

Someone was now following *him!*

He grinned as he raced along.

So there'd been two of them, had there? And they'd decided to play on him the old sandwich trick that had harassed so many pavement-pounding cops. It was so simple. You gave A a reason for chasing B, and then started C chasing after A. In theory, A should stop to let his pursuer catch up. And at that point, both sides of the sandwich, B and C, would gently melt away into thin air, and leave A waiting, and waiting.

But this particular A, Asey thought, wasn't going to fall for such tactics. This A intended to keep going after B, and catch him!

He couldn't miss catching the fellow, now. For all the twisting and turning, Asey knew just where he was headed. In just about two shakes of a lamb's tail, the pine woods would end and the Pogue marsh would begin. Only an outlander would ever head toward that marsh, and only a fool would ever try to cross it. Being both, B was going to get caught, if not in the marsh itself, then in the curve between the inlet and the salt pond. B didn't stand a chance of getting away.

But Asey's optimism suffered a rude shock as he reached the edge of the woods and found the Pogue marsh stretching out ahead, empty.

The shore on either side of him was empty, too.

"Huh!" Asey paused and considered the situation. "He certainly didn't have time to dig himself any little foxholes to crawl—oho, the old bridge! That's the answer!"

The fellow couldn't have crossed over the few battered remaining planks of the bridge that had once spanned the old herring creek, or he'd still be in sight, floundering in the mud on the other side.

He must be hiding under it!

He had to be, Asey thought as he tiptoed over toward it, came to a halt a few feet away, and very cautiously stooped down to investigate.

Nobody was crouching there in the thick, mucilaginous mud of the creek bottom.

But as he started to straighten up, something like a ton of bricks fell on him.

The fellow had been watching him all the time, had sneaked under the bridge to the other side, swung up on it, and jumped him from above.

Asey figured out that eminently reasonable conclusion as he went thudding down into the muck.

Before he could make any attempt to rise, his right arm was pinned back against his head, forcing his face down deeper into the black glue. His legs and ankles felt as if they were being sat on by several Porter Supertanks.

He gathered himself together to break the holds—not for nothing had he spent so many spare hours learning the modern tricks of the Porter Plant guards!

But the man pinning him down had apparently forgotten more than the Porter guards' teacher had ever known. All Asey's inspired strugglings only seemed to aid his captor in dragging him under the bridge, and tying him up in a few more knots.

Now he could hear the sound of heavy footsteps back in the pine woods—that, Asey thought, would be the person who'd been chasing him, and who must somehow have got lost or delayed in the shuffle.

The person clumped around noisily on the shore for several moments.

Then the footsteps thumped away.

Everything was quiet again except for the shrill screeching of the sea gulls over by the inlet, and the labored, bubbling sound that was his own attempt to breathe without being suffocated in the slime.

Suddenly he was picked up like a baby and lifted out from under the bridge.

He never got even a glimpse of the man's face as he felt himself sailing through the air like a beanbag. There was only a vague, confused blur of someone in dark clothes, already starting to run.

Then he hit the mudhole.

Five minutes later, he had managed to clean his eyes out enough to see dimly, and by sheer luck he had located one shoe.

After groping for a solid quarter of an hour, he found the other.

Holding the somewhat gruesome objects by their laces, he wearily set off back through the pines. There was no sense in attempting to put them on, or to clean himself off. You couldn't with your bare hands tackle mud like this mud, which had been several centuries in the process of formation!

Hanson could figure out what all this business meant. He couldn't, himself.

All he knew was that he'd probably guessed wrong once more. B and C couldn't have been teamed up in any sandwich act, if B had taken such pains to hide from C under the bridge!

"Maybe," he muttered in disgust, "they're just testin' out a new kind of postwar hide an' seek. Maybe they're writin' a book about games!"

He wasn't a whit surprised, on returning to the still figure on the path, to find that the rosebud plate and the cod line had vanished from the branches of the pine seedling. He almost really hadn't expected them to be there.

In fact, he wouldn't even have blinked if the body had been spirited away. A missing corpse would have been just about all this crazy affair needed for a finishing touch.

He turned and padded off in his muddy stocking feet down toward the shore, to proceed with his original intention of getting someone to telephone Dr. Cummings for him.

But the beach which earlier had been so densely populated and so bustling with activity was now quite bare and empty.

As far as he could see, there was nothing but hurricane debris. A few sea gulls and sandpeep provided the only living note.

Asey told himself that after all, if anyone had wanted to move the girl or take her away, they'd had ample opportunity when they took the plate and the line. He might as well return to Junior and run over to the doctor's in person.

Then, he mentally added, he'd go home and change his clothes. The chill wind that was now starting to drive in from the east reminded him forcibly that he couldn't hang around forever in this slimy, sodden state. Now that the mud was beginning to harden, he was feeling more and more like a clammy statue of wet plaster of Paris.

Glancing over toward the shore road, he noticed that the red jeep was still where he had left it.

That was good, he thought, because in his excitement on first viewing the inlet beach, he had carelessly left the key in the ignition, and yesterday's experiences with small boys and curious onlookers had proved the danger of such negligence. Junior was a magnet. People couldn't somehow quite manage to keep their hands off him. Not in the sense that they wished to steal him permanently. They simply wanted to drive him, to try him out. "If only just around the block," as that elderly woman in Pennsylvania had told him without a blush of shame when she finally returned Junior to the parking space of the roadside stand where he'd stopped for coffee.

New Englanders—and particularly Cape Codders—had more restraint, he decided.

Even the blonde girl in green slacks and tan windbreaker who'd just rounded a curve in the road was only stopping and staring. While she was clearly admiring Junior, she wasn't climbing—

"Hey!" Asey opened his mud-caked lips and yelled out at the top of his lungs. "Hey—don't! No! Get *out* of that! Hey, don't—"

But the blonde girl had hopped lightly behind the wheel, started Junior, and was already bouncing off down the road.

"The next hundred an' ninety-eight words," Asey sounded as annoyed as he felt, "have been cut out by the censor! What is this, Kick-Mayo-in-the-Face Day, for Pete's sakes? Can't anything work out right? Can't anything go straight?"

Hunching his shoulders and jamming his hands into his mud-filled pockets, he headed grimly into the wind-swept stretch.

It was really blowing now, the sun had disappeared behind sullen gray clouds, the inlet surface was like pale steel, and Asey felt less and less like a plaster of Paris statue and more and more like a cake of ice.

He looked up hopefully at the sound of an oncoming car speeding toward him from the village.

But it wasn't Junior being returned, only a somewhat rackety black sedan.

Asey raised his hand and hailed it anyway.

After all, Cummings should be phoned before any more time got frittered away. This person could attend to the call as well as anyone else. He also thought that anyone with an ounce of human charity would probably take pity on him and drive him home before he congealed.

When the driver showed no inclination to stop at his violent hand waving, Asey stepped out directly into the center of the road.

Reluctantly, amid the protests of mournfully squealing brakes, the car jolted to a halt. Its driver and only occupant, a sharp-faced, black-haired woman, darted a nervous glance at him, and then hurriedly reached back and rather obviously pushed the car door lock down with one finger.

As Asey walked up to speak to her, he could hear the squeaking of the window being rolled up tight to the top.

He wondered irritably what the matter was with her. What in time did she take him for, anyway, a tramp with evil intentions?

A brief glance at his mud-smudged, frowning face as he passed by the side-wing mirror reminded him that she had no particular reason to take him for much of anything else. Indeed, under the circumstances, "tramp" was almost a tag of kindness.

Her long thin face and aquiline nose were familiar to him. She was someone Jennie knew.

He searched his memory with desperate haste. She lived in the gray clapboard salt-box house on the inlet road, the one that used to belong to Bill Larkin. She took summer boarders, and her brother had a little boat yard. Out in front of her house there were always wooden racks filled with beachplum jelly to sell to the tourist trade. Jennie had always sniffed at the display, and muttered scornful things about artificial colorings and commercial pectins, and maybe one old beachplum having been waved across the kitchen for flavor.

"Curran!" he said triumphantly. "Miss Curran, isn't it? I'm Asey Mayo. Jennie Mayo's cousin, you know."

No sign of any enthusiastic recognition flashed across her sharp features. In fact, she looked as if she hadn't heard a single word. She actually hadn't, Asey suddenly realized, what with being bottled up inside the car as she was, with the windows closed tight, and the wind blowing.

He raised his voice and yelled.

Miss Curran sat there with pursed lips, looking straight ahead.

Asey put his mouth up close to the glass and fairly howled.

"Mayo! Mayo! Jennie's cousin! Asey *Mayo*—look, open the window a bit, will you, *please?*"

By the time she broke down to the extent of unwinding the window a fraction of an inch, Asey's tired voice had turned into a hoarse croak.

At the sound of it, Miss Curran looked even more worried, and started to wind the window up to the top once more.

"Look, all I want is for you to make a phone call for me!" Asey said hurriedly. "Will you do that, please? It's important!"

Miss Curran shook her head.

Asey fished around in his pockets till he unearthed a quarter. After wiping off the mud, he edged it through the narrow open gap at the top of the window, and let it fall down inside.

"There's the money for the call," he said. "Keep the change. Just you phone—"

He broke off as Miss Curran bent down and started fumbling on the floor of the car.

After a moment she found the quarter and flipped it back at him through the window crack.

"No phone," she said coldly.

"Well," Asey tried not to sound too annoyed or too impatient, "well, if you haven't got a phone—"

"I have."

"Well, Miss Curran, if you don't feel like usin' yours, d'you suppose you might possibly be willin' to stop at the next house, maybe, an' phone for me from there? I don't like to bother you, but—"

"There isn't any phone in the next house, or the next, or the next," Miss Curran said with finality.

"Oh, come!" Asey said. "There certainly *are* phones in this vicinity—oh. I forgot. Hurricane trouble, of course!"

"They're working on 'em," Miss Curran said. "They think *maybe* Tuesday. Of course, I'd be glad to phone for you then."

"D'you suppose," Asey said as she started up the car, "that you'd be willin' to drive me back to the village so I could phone from there?"

She eyed his clothes, and then she eyed the car's upholstery.

She didn't actually come right out and say no. She didn't have to.

"Look," Asey said a little desperately, "this *is* important, Miss Curran. I've found the body of a dead girl over yonder in the inlet woods, an' I want to get to a phone an'—"

"I told you, there aren't any around here!" she interrupted.

"I want to phone the doctor!" Asey finished up.

"There isn't any," Miss Curran informed him.

"*What?*"

"I said, there isn't any. No doctor."

"If only," Asey said, "I could make you believe me! I know I look like the tramp in the nightmare, but I *am* Asey Mayo, an' I *did* find this girl, an' I *do* want to phone Cummings an' have him—"

"I know, I know, I heard you!" Miss Curran broke in. "And I've told you a million times, *no* phones! *And* no doctor, either. Cummings isn't here. He isn't in town. He isn't *home!*"

"He's never what you really might call home," Asey said. "He's always sort of en route, like. I know. But here I am on the shore, three miles from the village, shiverin' from head to foot with cold mud—hear my teeth chatterin'? An' before it gets dark, I want to get hold of the doc an' have him get to that girl!"

"Cummings," Miss Curran said, "has left town. He's gone away. He isn't *here*. He's on a *vacation! Va-ca-tion!* I certainly can't make it any plainer than that!"

She threw the car into gear quickly, and the sedan sped off up the road.

Two hours later, Asey stalked into his own kitchen, marched through to the dining room, mounted the back stairs, and made a beeline for the bathtub.

The sound of running water brought Jennie hurrying up from the parlor to the back hall.

"Asey, is that *you?* Where've you *been?* Did you find the blinds? Isn't it perfectly awful along the inlet there? Asey! Asey—oh, bother!"

But the rush of running water thwarted her only temporarily. When it gave way to simple splashing, she took a stand outside the bathroom door and proceeded to get him caught up on the state of domestic affairs.

"Asey, it was a perfectly *won*derful sale—d'you hear me? We got a hundred and sixty-two dollars from the sale itself! *Think* of it! And forty-seven-fifty in just contributions—just for fun, because I really didn't think anyone *would,* you see, I put that big decorated flower pot on the front steps with a sign over it sayin' PUT YOUR CONTRIBUTIONS IN HERE. And they *did!* And then we got three-seventy-five from Mildred's hurricane postcards. And," she sounded a little breathless, *"and* two hundred and fifty dollars more from our donated antique—you hear that, Asey?"

"I hear."

"Don't you want to know *who* donated the antique?" Jennie asked eagerly. "Asey, are you listenin' to me? Don't you want to know *who?"*

"Who?" Asey asked obediently, although he didn't care very much.

"You did! It was that old cherry table you had down in the boathouse, the one you keep fishin' tackle on. Well, I sanded it down and fixed up the legs, last week, and that antique-collectin' friend of Mrs. Berry's, she asked if I'd take two-fifty for it. I must say I hesitated, because I'd finished it pretty good, and *I* thought it was worth more than two dollars and fifty cents! *I* thought *ten,* myself. Then she said she'd seen better ones for two *hundred—* *well,* I tell you, I was flabbergasted, but I never let on! I told her I'd *hoped* to get more, and I made up this woman in Orleans who thought *she* wanted it, and was willin' to pay *any*way two-fifty—"

Jennie covered the donated antique deal down to the last minute detail.

"So when she said she'd write a check, I thought quick! If she got that cherry table home and didn't *like* it, she *might* stop the check! So I said would she mind awfully lettin' me have cash if she happened to have it with her—what's that?"

"I said, would you mind awfully gettin' me my clothes, please? The works. Shoes, too."

A moment later, Jennie passed them in to him.

"And when she opened her bag, Asey, and took out her billfold, I realized how dumb I'd been! I could have cried! Why, she'd have paid me twice that! I never saw so many new ten dollar bills in all my life! Crisp, brand-new ten dollar bills—you say somethin'?"

"I sighed," Asey said.

"So she forked over twenty-five of 'em, and if you'll let me have it, I think maybe I'll fix up that old busted sea chest in the attic—the one with the bad hinges—and see if I can't palm that off on her. Asey, there isn't a *speck* of food left except for an old pudding that didn't get called for. I'm sort of afraid you've either got to have eggs for supper, or else take us to Howard Johnson's. If only you'd let me *know* you were comin', I'd have had a nice meal ready for you! I *did* save out some more apple turnovers, but somebody found 'em and sold 'em—Asey, that plate! That rosebud plate!"

"Rosebud plate?"

Asey's voice sounded so strangely muffled, Jennie decided he must be putting on his shirt.

"I *do* hope you brought that plate back! You did, didn't you? I never should have let you take it in the first place, but you whipped out of that window so quick, I didn't have a chance to—"

She broke off as he came out into the hall, and pointed to the muddy mess in his hand.

"Goodness gracious, what's *that?* Ugh!"

"Wa-el," Asey drawled, "I don't know just what you *would* call it, now. You ever hear tell of a torture they called the Iron Maiden, a kind of an iron suit lined with long spikes that they used to tuck people into years ago, an' shut 'em up in? For the last two hours, this mess has been a sort of Iron Maiden without spikes for me. Before that, it was my best suit. I used to save it for Porter directors' meetin's. I almost felt like a Porter director when I was dressed up in it."

"I never saw the *like,* never!" Jennie said in horror. "What're you goin' to *do* with it now?"

"Put it out in the woodshed," Asey told her, "an' hope that some benevolent wood sprite'll sneak it away so's I'll never have to set eye on it again."

"What've you been *do*in', anyway?" Jennie demanded as she followed him down the back stairs. "Where've you *been?* Why, those clothes look as if you'd got tossed into some stank old mud-hole out on the marsh!"

"I was."

Jennie stared at him skeptically as he snapped on the dining-room light. "Hm. You were, were you?"

"Uh-huh. I was."

She sniffed. "All right, all right, if you don't *want* to let me know what happened, why, *don't* tell me! But it still looks—and I must say it *smells*—as if you'd got tossed into an old marsh mudhole! What about that rosebud plate, Asey? Did you bring it back?"

"Was it one of ours?" he countered with another question as he entered the kitchen.

"No, that's just the point! It belongs to that Mrs. Peeling—she's a writer, and she bought the Martin place last spring. Honestly, I don't know what I'll *do* if you've gone and lost that plate some-where! Mrs. Peeling's spent years gettin' a full set of that old pink rosebud pattern—goodness knows why, I'm sure!" she added. "Grandmother Hopkins had a set of it, and she got so tired of hers, she took it out behind the barn one day and smashed it up. Every-one used to have one of those sets, you know. They were *the* thing to have. Some minister's widow in Wellfleet painted 'em all by hand. Anyway, when this Mrs. Peeling brought her turnovers, she said she hadn't meant to leave 'em on that plate, and would I please be awful careful of it. So *don't* tell me you've gone and left it anywhere! Just don't *tell* me!"

"All right, I won't. But I wish you'd tell *me*," Asey paused with his hand on the woodshed doorknob, "why you never mentioned that Cummings had gone away on a vacation!"

"Why, I only heard about it myself this mornin'— Mary told me when she came. Seems some nephew doctor of his that used to be in the navy is takin' his place. Honest, I can't imagine what must have come over the doctor, can you?"

Asey shook his head. "Nope, an' I can't imagine why it had to come over him at this particular time, either. What happened to the man? Did he just up an' go?"

"Mary said she heard that he called his wife into his office, and said he was fed up, they were goin' off on a trip, and for her to pack quick. Said this nephew that had dropped down that mornin' from Boston, he'd stay an' take over for him, though he'd only intended just to spend the day. And so off they went, yesterday afternoon. Just like that!"

"You don't think anything's the matter with the doc, do you?" Asey inquired. "He isn't sick, or anything? Of course, once in a while he's threatened to do somethin' like this, but I never knew him to actually go off on a vacation before, ever!"

"He never *did!* Why, more'n once his wife's got so mad, she's flounced off by herself for a few weeks. You know that. *No*body knows what got into the man now. Mary says this nephew—his name's Horner—he's supposed to be wonderful. Got a lot of medals for what he did for wounded men, and all. But she said that she caught a glimpse of him in the drugstore this mornin', and he looked awful young, like. Like a child, sort of."

"Mary almost put her finger on it," Asey said. "I'd say, like a stupid child."

"Have *you* seen him?"

"Yes-yes. Yes, indeed," Asey said. "I've seen young Dr. Horner. My, my, yes!"

"Asey, somethin's happened! I been thinkin' so since I seen those clothes, and now I know it! What's been goin' on? Why'd you go to see Horner? What happened this afternoon?"

"Wa-el," Asey said, "reduced to its lowest terms, I went blind huntin', as per your orders."

"What happened? Did you find 'em?"

Asey turned away from the door and looked at her thoughtfully before answering.

Then he shook his head.

"It doesn't seem to matter how often I try to tell it to people," he said at last. "Even to me, it still sounds plumb, stark crazy. Listen, while I was huntin' blinds in the inlet woods, I come on this piece of cod line, an' reeled it up over that rosebud plate. An' after a while, I reeled my way along through the pines straight to the body of a girl—"

"Asey!" Jennie said in horror. "You *never* did! *Who?* Who was she? What happened?"

"I'm not goin' to tell you what happened to *me*," Asey said, "from the time I found her till I finally managed to hitchhike a ride to town. I want to forget that period of my life. As to what happened to *her*—wa-el, young Dr. Kildare there—what's his name, Horner? Horner first decided it was an accident. He said she'd just tripped, or fallen, that was all. But upon havin' my contrary point of view thrown at him sort of forcible—I was so cold an' uncomfortable in my mud pack, I guess I was a lot more forcible than I meant to be. Anyway, Horner backed water considerable, said that was only his first snap judgment, and finally he agreed that yes, the girl had been killed. We got the fact established clinically. The girl'd been hit very expert, you see. Rabbit punch."

"*Who* was she?" Jennie's voice seemed to have gone up an octave. "*Who* was she?"

"Search me. Horner doesn't know anyone around—he wasn't any help in identifyin' her. An' Hanson'd never seen her before— it was just dumb luck, stumblin' on Hanson uptown. He was investigatin' some reports on lootin'. They were still tryin' to find out her name when I left an' hitched a ride home—I was near frozen to death by then. She—say, have we got a new cat, or has Big Joe taken to havin' fits out in the shed? I never heard such queer sounds as those comin'—"

"Bother the cat!" Jennie stepped between him and the door. "Bother the sounds! I want to know *who* that girl was!"

"But I can't tell you, I don't—"

"I *got* to know!" Jennie said breathlessly. "I *got* to! Tell me quick, what did she look like?"

"Oh, she was young, an' slim, medium height, expensively dressed—"

"Did she have a streak of white in her hair?" Jennie clutched at his arm and shook it in her excitement. "Did she?"

"Yes." Asey reached past her, and shoved open the shed door as more odd noises issued from the place. "Yes, she did. Why are you so awful—"

He stopped.

His indomitable cousin Jennie had slumped down at his feet on the kitchen floor, in a dead faint.

THREE

ASEY stood and looked blankly down at her, completely ignoring the odd noises and strange crashes that still issued from the shed.

Even the sound of the shed door being forced open didn't move him.

He'd guessed all along that someone was prowling around out there. Those hadn't been four-footed as much as two-footed noises.

But even if the whole shed had crashed down on a regiment of prowlers, he wouldn't have stirred.

He was simply too dumbfounded to move.

Other women could faint like flies, and it wouldn't signify a thing. But when Jennie keeled over, *that* was something to date things by!

Feeling both dazed and inadequate, he went hesitantly over to the sink and drew a glass of water.

Then, after a long moment of uncertainty, he came back to Jennie and knelt down on the floor beside her.

"Didn't you ever take first aid?"

Asey spilled half the water on the floor as he jerked around.

The blonde girl in green slacks and tan windbreaker had just pushed open the kitchen door leading from the back yard.

"Didn't you ever take first aid?" she repeated somewhat sharply. "You shouldn't *raise* her head!"

Asey gently guided Jennie's head back onto the checked linoleum.

The probable return of Junior had nothing whatever to do with his sudden feeling of relief, and Asey frankly admitted the fact to himself. It was the mere presence of a third person which seemed to make everything a lot brighter.

"Hullo," he said. "Did you bring Junior back?"

"You mean the jeep? Yes. It's down the lane. I've had a simply morbid time finding out who you were and where you lived—look, I simply cannot bear this! You're doing things all upside down! Leave her head alone, and *don't* try to make her drink—oh, *do* move out of the way and let me see to things! You're *all* wrong!"

"When I'm faced with a situation that's all upside down an' wrong," Asey returned, "I believe in applyin' similar methods as a cure. My cousin Jennie never fainted in her life!"

"Could be. But she certainly has now!" The girl bent down and felt Jennie's pulse professionally. "Go get some pillows to put under her legs—oh, got any smelling salts? Never mind—I see some ammonia by the sink. Hurry up with those pillows!"

Asey hurried up with them.

After arranging them to the girl's satisfaction, he stepped out into the shed, snapped on the light, and looked around.

Along with most of Jennie's own household tool assortment, the kindling pile was now scattered all over the floor.

That was what the prowler had dislodged, and been forced to wade through before he succeeded in groping his way to the door and getting it open.

Asey surveyed the girl curiously as he returned to the kitchen.

Had she been out there in the shed, and then run around to the side door?

The timing, he thought, was just about right.

She must originally have come into the kitchen, and then slipped into the shed when she heard him and Jennie coming down the stairs. That would account for her having such difficulties in locating the door. Anyone who'd entered by it wouldn't have run into such problems finding it again.

"Say, what were you doin' out in the shed just now?" he asked casually.

"Shed?" she raised her eyebrows and looked up at him. "What shed?"

"Mine. Weren't you roamin' around out there a few minutes ago?"

"Why, no—what an odd idea for you to have! I haven't been

roaming in your shed—or anyone else's, for that matter—although I've roamed virtually everywhere else, hunting you!"

"Are you quite sure about that?" Asey persisted. "Far be it from me to seem to doubt your word, but the circumstantial evidence is kind of strong, like."

"I can't help your circumstantial evidence!" the girl retorted. "I certainly ought to know best where I've been, and I *wasn't* in your shed! I came up the lane to your kitchen door—I knocked, but you apparently didn't hear me, so I just barged in. She's coming around all right," she patted Jennie's shoulder. "She's beginning to snap out of it—or don't you care? You don't seem very interested in the poor woman!"

Asey bit his lip. Unquestionably, the girl had been very helpful. She was still so obviously concerned about Jennie's condition, he didn't want to come right out and say that his cousin had been shamming like mad for at least the last two minutes!

"Of course I'm interested," he said aloud. "Only it looked to me like she was perkin' up. Where'd you say Junior was?"

"Down at the fork. That network of lanes confused me so, I left it back there. Truly, I'd never have dared to take that jeep if I'd known it belonged to you, Mr. Mayo!" she said contritely. "I thought you drove a Porter Bullet roadster that looked like a robot bomb. I wouldn't have *touched* it if I'd recognized you when you yelled at me, back on the shore road. The trouble was, you weren't dressed properly!"

"There's somethin' about makin' intimate connections with a mudhole," Asey told her, "that sort of takes the edge off the well-dressed man."

"What I mean is, *now* you look like the rotogravure pictures of yourself—corduroys and flannel shirt and yachting cap, and all. I'd recognize you anywhere in the outfit you're wearing now! There, there!" she patted Jennie's shoulder again, "take it easy, you're all right! You see, Mr. Mayo, I simply couldn't resist your jeep!"

"So I gathered," Asey said dryly.

The girl's face turned very pink. "You don't exactly make it simple for people to explain things, do you?" she asked. "But I'm going to tell you, anyway. I used to be a Wac, and when I saw that dear little red jeep, I just got completely carried away. I didn't really intend to steal it—"

"Just for old times' sakes," Asey broke in and finished her sentence for her, "you wanted to drive it around the block. Uh-huh."

"How—how did you know that was what I was going to say?"

"It's what the ex-soldier in Providence said when he borrowed Junior temporarily, an' what the ex-Wave said, an' so on. You're not the first person to be tempted by Junior."

"Well, I'm very ashamed of myself, now, and very apologetic. I shouldn't have touched it—you've fixed it up lots, haven't you? It's very refined. That seat job's particularly good—there, there, lamb pie," she said to Jennie, "don't try to talk, just lie there quietly! No, no, don't say a *word!* Just keep nice and still for a few moments!"

Asey grinned. "You may know all the rules," he said, "but I know my cousin! Go on, Jennie, talk! What's wrong?"

"Don't encourage her, Mr. Mayo! She simply shouldn't talk! She ought to lie quietly—"

"If you try to keep her from talkin' when she wants to," Asey said, "she'll most likely suffer a terrible bad relapse. What was wrong, Jennie?"

He knew that she knew who the dead girl was, and that the shock of identification had been entirely genuine. He knew, too, that she'd delayed what might be called her official coming-to until she'd got the situation cleared up and straightened out in her mind. He couldn't imagine what was coming, but he mentally braced himself for almost anything.

"Get me up!" Jennie said. "And *do* stop pattin' me like a dog—"

"But you must lie there!"

Jennie shook off the girl's restraining hand and struggled up to a sitting position.

"I'm not spendin' any more time on this cold linoleum! Help me over to a chair, Asey. I feel like an awful old fool—but to have *this* happen, after the way I worked, and worked, and *worked!*"

"You've had a tough day," Asey said sympathetically, thinking of course that she was referring to her labors on behalf of the Women's Club. "I hadn't any business to spring the mess on you the way I did. I'm sorry. I shouldn't have—"

He broke off under the force of Jennie's baleful stare.

"To think how I *worked!*" she shook her head sadly. "To think how *hard* I worked on you!"

"On *me?*"

"I never worked so hard on anybody in my born days as I worked to—" Jennie suddenly closed her lips tightly together.

The action puzzled Asey. He'd seen clams snap their shells together in much the same way, but Jennie wasn't particularly renowned for her clamlike tendencies. On the contrariwise.

It was the presence of the blonde girl that was gagging her, he realized as Jennie turned to her with her lips curved up into a company smile.

"You're Mrs. Peeling's sister, aren't you? I suppose she sent you to get that rosebud plate. But you tell her I'm goin' to wait till mornin' to take it back to her myself, will you? Because," Jennie said brightly, "I—uh—I'm goin' to take her a little surprise on it. I'm sure it was real kind of you to help Asey look after me—men are so sort of stupid when anyone faints! It was real nice of you to take the time to bother, and thank you very, very much. That plate'll get returned first thing in the mornin', Miss Peeling."

It wasn't, Asey thought, the sort of speech Jennie made very often. Her methods were ordinarily more direct. If she wanted to dismiss someone, she didn't make any bones about it.

But even though she continued to look brightly expectant, he knew she was annoyed when the girl made no move to depart.

"I'm Mrs. Peeling's sister, but my name is Cook," she said. "Lois Cook. I'm afraid I don't really know what you mean about a plate. With shame oozing from every pore, I have to confess I was returning Mr. Mayo's jeep, which I stole, to put it baldly. Now I've returned it, I'm stranded. I could walk home, but it's cold, and I really don't know my way around these lanes at night—may I phone for the village taxi to come and get me? That is, if your phone's working."

"Show her where the phone is, Asey!" Jennie said briskly, without even murmuring a polite suggestion that Asey drive her home.

She carefully closed the door behind him when he returned alone to the kitchen.

"I didn't recognize that girl at first, and I didn't want to say much while she was around. Oh, honest, I could cry when I think how hard I worked on you!"

"What *are* you talkin' about?" Asey demanded. "Worked on me for *what*?"

"To get rid of you, of course! To get you out of the way! To get you out of this house this afternoon, so you'd never see her! She was leavin' town tomorrow, and didn't know when she'd be back —in fact, she'd been thinkin' serious of sellin' her place here, and not comin' back at all! If you didn't run into her here, this afternoon, the chances was you'd *never* met her. Oh, oh, oh! How can such perfectly awful things happen!"

"I don't get any of this!" Asey thought he'd never seen such anguish on his cousin's face. "Will you just go slow, an' remember that I don't even know yet who this girl was? Now tell me—who was—"

"I didn't worry a mite when she didn't show up at the lawn fête," Jennie went on mournfully. "I was almost glad she didn't, though goodness knows we could have used any money she cared to spend!—it was really *her* I thought might fall for that little cherry table! I kept thinkin' to myself that as long as *she* wasn't here, anyway I wouldn't have to be on pins and needles for fear *you'd* come larrupin' back and run into her!"

"Who," Asey asked with firmness as she stopped for breath, "who *was* the gir—"

"Well, all I can say is," Jennie concluded in the bleakly resigned tones of a condemned woman, "this is one perfectly awful mess, and I hate to face it!"

Asey nodded. "I came to that same conclusion myself," he informed her. "I told Hanson I washed my hands of it, when he asked me to help him. He'd have managed all right if I wasn't here. He an' Little Lord Fauntleroy—that Horner fellow—they can work it out between 'em. After my life with that cod line an' the mud pack, I reminded myself I'd come home for a rest, an' I mean to have one. So if it's my part in this that's worryin' you, don't worry any longer. Except for wantin' to know who the girl is, I'm not botherin' with this one. I'm sittin' it out."

"Is that so, Mister Codfish Sherlock?" Jennie inquired in her most withering tones. "Is that *so?* Well, let me tell you, this's one you're goin' to sit in on, and quick! You're goin' to solve this one faster than you ever solved anything before in your life!"

"What?" Asey stared at her. "What's the matter with you? Why've I got to do any such thing? Look here, who *was* the girl? What's all this to-do about, anyway?"

"You didn't recognize her, truly?"

"Why, I thought there was somethin' sort of familiar about her," Asey started to fill his pipe, "but that's all! Was she someone I used to know when she was a kid? One of that gang I used to give sailin' lessons to at the club, years ago?"

Jennie's sigh sounded rather like a factory siren.

"So you really don't know! Asey, I almost can't believe you, and I'm sure nobody else will! Oh, you know her! You *must!*"

"I tell you I don't!" Asey retorted. "I don't know what all this mystery's about! When I first saw her face, I'll admit I had a feelin' of havin' known someone who looked like her. But what is there in that, I'd like to know, to make you stew around keepin' me from her, all dramatic-like? Why should you swoon, all dramatic-like? What goes on? Who was she?"

He strode across to the old iron match safe by the stove, impatiently jabbed a match against the worn piece of sandpaper tacked to the wall underneath it, and held the match up to the bowl of his pipe.

"I s'pose," Jennie said slowly, "that you remember King Tinsbury, don't you?"

She could see that the match was burning into the palm of Asey's hand. But even though he was looking down at the flame, he didn't seem to be aware of it.

"Yes," he said at last. "I remember him. What's that got to do with this girl?"

"Only that she was Ann Tinsbury, King's daughter," Jennie told him. "That's all!"

Asey turned and tossed the charred match stem into the sink.

"I'm very sorry for her," he said. "She was a lovely lookin' girl. I'm sure she never deserved what happened to her. But I'm still not sorry I told Hanson I wasn't havin' anything to do with this affair, an' I still can't imagine why you think I should. Tell me, whenever did King Tinsbury come back to town?"

"Last spring. He died in August of a heart attack. I didn't write you anything about it, because—well," Jennie said with a shrug, "I thought I'd just wait and see. They told me he'd grown awful flighty and eccentric. Never stayed anywhere very long. They said he had kind of a hobby of buyin' big houses, changin' 'em over, and then movin' on to another. The way he switched the Callendar place around, you'd never recognize it!"

"That old ark beyond the inlet? With all the porches an' columns an' balconies?"

Jennie nodded. "He had all of 'em stripped off till it looks halfway between a cow barn and an old shoe. Ann was away when he died, but she came back last month. She was a nice girl, Asey. *I* liked her!"

"She looked like a nice girl. I'm sure she was if you liked her."

He didn't mean to sound perfunctory about it. Almost automatically, as Jennie launched into an enthusiastic discussion of Ann Tinsbury, he found himself figuring out the girl's probable route from Callendar's, beyond the inlet woods, to his own house and the lawn fête.

He guessed that she would have taken that path from its very start. It should be no chore for Hanson to check up on her progress along it, considering the crowd on the shore.

"So you see, she was in Europe when the war broke out, and all durin' it," Jennie was saying. "She worked with the Quakers, and the Red Cross, and other relief outfits. She was taken prisoner by the Italians, and got away, and she didn't come home till she heard about her father—" she paused. "You look like you were thinkin' hard. I hope you've stopped pretendin' you don't know why you got to solve this quick!"

"I don't."

Jennie clucked her tongue in exasperation. "Oh, you must be puttin' it on! Don't tell me you've forgotten that night you beat King Tinsbury to a pulp, on Main Street, right in front of everybody? *I* remember! It's the only time I ever saw you mad clear through—your face was still black when you came thunderin' home here. Remember it, don't you?"

"Uh-huh. I remember." Asey sat down at the kitchen table, teetered the chair back against the wall, and laughed softly. "I *was* sore, I guess!"

"You *guess!* Can't you remember what you said? You said you didn't want to hear of King Tinsbury or think about him again, and never to mention his name in your presence!"

"Golly, did I? I was pretty good an' sore," Asey said reminiscently. "Yessiree, I was *mad!* He'd swiped some of old Cap'n Porter's blueprints, an' beat us to a couple of patents that was goin' to ruin the Porter Company overnight. An' there wasn't a thing we could try to do to him legal that wouldn't have taken so much time we'd have been sunk durin' it. 'Course, what riled me most was that he'd swiped them things from *me!*"

"I never thought it was your fault!" Jennie protested. "How was you to know what he was up to?"

"I didn't, but I'd ought to have guessed. I'll never forget the next month, with Porter an' old Mack an' the rest of us workin' like dogs! But when we got through, we had a new Porter engine no one's ever been able to beat in the thirty-odd years since." He chuckled. "Yessir, I'll always remember that month, but I'd almost forgotten that fight with King."

"Maybe you have," Jennie said sharply, "but no one else around this town ever has, or ever will!"

"Oh, sure they have! They forgot it just as soon as they had somethin' else new to talk about," Asey said. "Like some other cake sale or lawn fête, or somebody's paintin' a picket fence a different color. Why, no one ever mentioned a word about that fight to me afterwards!"

"Who'd have *dared* to?" Jennie demanded. "Nobody! Not after you'd ordered 'em not to, in your worst quarter-deck bellow! But you know," she added, "you *did* say if you ever saw King Tinsbury in this town again, you'd kill him! You stood there on Main Street and yelled it out at the top of your lungs!"

"I'm sure I did," Asey returned. "I bet I meant every syllable of it, too. But what's that old story got to do with King's daughter?"

"You didn't just stop with threatening King, Asey Mayo, and you know it! You covered a lot of territory. You said you'd kill him, or—" she hesitated. "Well, you said it! You said him, or any of his *family!*"

"Now see here, Jennie!" Asey stopped teetering his chair, and sat up very straight at the table. "Just because I let go at someone in the heat of anger thirty years ago, or more—why, I don't suppose I've thought of King Tinsbury a dozen times since! I been too busy! Besides, the way things worked out, King really done Porter Motors a great favor!"

"That so? Hm. Best friend Porter Motors ever had, I s'pose," Jennie remarked with irony. "Best friend *you* ever had. Love birds, that's what!"

"Of course we thought the world was lost when we found out what King'd done!" Asey said. "Sure we did. But it turned out that our world had been awful small, an' that there was a lot more beyond it than we'd ever dreamed of till King forced our eyes open. Maybe I did threaten him, an' his children, an' his sisters, an' his cousins, an' his aunts, an' all his dogs an' cats, too. But you certainly can't think that means *I* had anything to do with his daughter bein' killed today!"

"*I* don't, no! Only the minute those women saw you this afternoon, when we was streamin' up from the boathouse, two of 'em behind me said, 'Oh, oh, what'll we *do!* And Ann Tinsbury's comin'!' "

"That's just plain silly," Asey said. "What I may have threatened him with never bothered King Tinsbury—I never happened to see him afterwards, but he often ran into the Porter family. D'you think if he'd taken me seriously, he'd have come back here, ever?"

"I know he left town the night of that fight," Jennie said. "And when he come back last spring, he had watchdogs with him, and two chauffeurs—big bruisers with cauliflower ears. Nobody ever called 'em bodyguards, but they were, all the same. Yes, yes, I know," she went on quickly as Asey started to speak, "you been away a lot. You've done so many things and seen so many people, you've got a different slant on all this business. P'r'aps you *have* almost forgotten it. Only other folks around here haven't. They remember!"

"An' supposin' they do? What *of* it?" Asey wanted to know.

"They'll go trottin' off and tell Hanson. Then it'll get into the newspapers. That's what of it!"

"Huh," Asey said with a chuckle, "it'd be a field day for 'em, wouldn't it? 'UNEXPECTED RETURN OF CODFISH SHERLOCK RESULTS IN MURDER OF OLD ENEMY'S BEAUTIFUL DAUGHTER.' 'NATIVES RECALL MAYO'S DIRE THREATS TO TINSBURY FAMILY.' 'HAYSEED SLEUTH CLAIMS HE WAS ONLY HUNTING BLINDS IN MURDER WOODS.' 'REELING COD LINE ON ROSEBUD PLATE'—now I wonder if the papers could make anythin' out of that cod line? Might be worth lettin' 'em loose to find out!"

"What'd you do with the plate, anyway?" Jennie asked.

"As long as it was in my possession, I took splendid care of it. Where it is now, I wouldn't know. Jennie, you know I had nothin' to do with the death of the Tinsbury girl, don't you?"

"Yes, of course I know it! So will most everyone else know it, too, except for a few gossips. Now, I know you don't care two figs about gossip or headlines. Usually I don't think they matter much, either. But right now they do. The *real* reason you got to solve this is that if you don't, people will always whisper that it was because *you* killed Ann, yourself. That's the truth, and you know it in your heart, don't you? You might's well admit it. You got to sooner or later!"

Asey didn't admit it, but he couldn't deny it.

"It's silly!" he said. "Hang it, Jennie, it isn't rational! It isn't sensible!"

"Lots of things are silly and senseless, but they happen just the same!" Jennie returned. "Think of *me* faintin'! I kept tellin' myself it wouldn't turn out to be Ann that you'd stumbled on, but some other girl—goodness gracious, I forgot all about—" she nodded her head toward the dining-room door, and went through an elaborate pantomime of telephoning, *"her!"*

"So'd I," Asey said.

"Seems to me she's been an awful long while!" Jennie whispered. "It shouldn't take her most fifteen minutes just to call the taxi! Hm! Hm, I wonder!"

Jennie tiptoed over to the dining-room door and jerked it open quickly.

Then, with a look of disappointment on her face, she gently closed it again.

"I wondered if she mightn't be listenin'," she said in a low voice, "but she's still sittin' at the phone! Must be she's waitin' for the taxi to come back from somewheres, or else she's callin' one long distance from Boston! Don't say too much in front of her, Asey. Her sister was far from bein' a friend of Ann's. I got a lot of ideas about Mrs. Peeling that we're goin' to look into after we get this Cook girl out of the way. She seems pleasant enough—what'd she mean by sayin' she stole—"

Jennie broke off as the door opened, and the girl came hesitantly back into the kitchen.

"We was beginnin' to wonder if you'd got lost," Asey told her with a smile.

"I am, actually. At least, I'm sunk. I can't get the taxi. I can't reach my sister anywhere, either. Or Brian—that's Brian Lemoyne —he's working with her on some material. I've tried simply everywhere they're likely to be, and where the phones are working. I'll have to walk." She fumbled at the diagonal zipper opening of her windbreaker. "It really isn't too cold. Did Ann—I mean, is it actually true about Ann Tinsbury?"

"How'd you find out about her?" Jennie demanded.

"The phone operator said that was why I couldn't get the taxi— she told me it'd been commandeered as an ambulance. For Ann." Her fingers worked away nervously at the zipper. "The operator knew I was calling from here, of course, and she asked me what I'd heard about—about everything."

"Were you a friend of Ann Tinsbury's?"

As Asey asked the casual question, he asked himself what else the phone operator had told Miss Cook. The girl was restless, fidgety, ill at ease. While she'd looked at him before with open interest and frank curiosity, she was now very definitely avoiding his eye.

"We went to school together years ago, in Chicago. But I haven't seen very much of her since I've been here in town with my sister. Ann and Maggie didn't—" she stopped working at the zipper and reached for a package of cigarettes in the sidepocket of her windbreaker. "Ann and Maggie moved in different groups. Maggie's more social, and less of a girl for causes. Ann was always going *at* things. Like her father. Did you," for the first time since she'd returned to the kitchen, Lois Cook turned and looked squarely at Asey, "did you ever happen to know King Tinsbury, Mr. Mayo?"

The challenge in that look and in her voice made Asey instantly realize that everything Jennie had been saying to him was the bitter truth. Already this girl had been told of the old Tinsbury fight, and of his threats to the whole Tinsbury family. That was what had made the noticeable difference in her attitude!

"Have a cookie!" Jennie said quickly. "Have a cookie—oh, I forgot! We sold 'em all. Well, suppose you wait till I get Asey a cup of coffee, and then I'll drive you home myself, in my car."

"Oh, no, thanks—I'll walk! A walk'll do me good. I don't get enough exercise." Lois was edging her way to the door. "And while I don't like to sound like your grandmother or anything, you know you're supposed to take things easy after what befell you! You shouldn't even think of driving!"

"Never havin' fainted before, I can't be expected to know what Mrs. Post thinks is proper," Jennie retorted. "I'm drivin' you. Asey can't. He's goin' to be too busy—you *are,* aren't you?"

Asey grinned.

"Sort of begins to look like maybe perhaps I am," he said. "I still think it's silly—but you win, cousin! I've got the point now!"

"Well, thank goodness you've made up your mind at last, an' *that's* all settled! Now we can speak a little more free, Miss Cook, because Asey'll have all this mess cleared right up in jig time. Yes, he knew King Tinsbury—and no matter what that gossipy little Eldredge chit told you over the phone, Asey never killed Ann! Why *think* of it! It's—it's—why it's just plain silly! So do stop shrinkin' around so, and sit down, and relax! I'll drive you home as soon's I've fed him. He isn't any old murderer, an' you don't have to run away from him like a scared little rabbit!"

"I wasn't!" Lois's face was scarlet with embarrassment. "Truly! I didn't believe her, anyway, really I didn't! Except she swore she'd just been talking with some state police officer, and she'd got the story straight from him! Otherwise I wouldn't—" she stopped as Asey started to laugh. "Oh, you've got me all mixed up, and I'm saying all the wrong things!"

"*See,* Asey?" Jennie said in triumph. "*Already!* It's just like I *told* you it'd be—wasn't any talk of arrestin' him, was there?" she asked Lois interestedly. "How far've they got?"

"Well," Lois wet her lips, "well—"

"Oh, go on, go on!" Jennie said. "Don't try to break it to us easy! What's the story?"

"Well, Myrna said there was some talk of the police finding a lobster pot buoy with Mr. Mayo's name on it, over in the woods quite near where Ann was found. They thought that it might have been used to hit her with."

"Good for Hanson!" Asey said approvingly. "I suggested he borrow some repair crew's floodlights so's he could see his way around to do a little scourin' of the vicinity right away. I'm glad he got goin'. A lobster pot buoy's a handy thing—at least, mine are. Just about the right weight, too, I'd say. An' it fits in fine with what Hanson knows of my movements. He could figger I'd picked the buoy up on the beach, an' was carryin' it convenient in my hand. Uh-huh, that's good! No talk about arrestin' me, though?"

Lois shook her head.

"Myrna didn't say anything about it to me. How—oh, how can you sit there, so—so—so unconcerned, and so—so—"

"Callous?" Asey suggested as he teetered back in his chair. "Wa-el, for years I've gone around blandly sayin' that a genuinely innocent man doesn't need to have any worries, an' now it seems like I been right. Jennie, I'd like some eggs to go with that coffee, please. An' some toast. An' I do wish you could have managed to hide out just one turnover!"

"It is a pity—you'll just have to smear jam on your toast an' pretend it's dessert! If—why, I *know* what!" Jennie said suddenly. "That puddin'! There won't be time to steam it up proper, but even cold it'll be better than nothin' at all! And there's some leftover hard sauce in the pantry, too. Yes, that's what we'll do, we'll have that pud—"

She paused in front of the electric refrigerator, got up on tiptoe, reached up both hands, and then turned around.

"What did you do with it, Asey?"

"Do with what?"

"The puddin', of course!"

"I didn't," Asey said. "Never saw it."

"Did you take it?" Jennie asked Lois.

"No, I didn't see it, either. Was it up on top of the refrigerator?"

"'It certainly was! I put it there myself a few minutes before you come home just now, Asey! With my own two hands, I put it up there—it had her name on it!"

"*Whose* name?" Asey inquired.

"Ann's. She'd ordered it. Now who, I'd like to know, *who's* stolen Ann Tinsbury's puddin'?"

FOUR

"Sure you didn't put it somewhere else?" Asey suggested.

"I guess I'm old enough to know where I put things! While you were takin' your bath, don't you remember I told you the only thing we had left from the sale was a puddin'? Not five minutes before then, I'd taken it off the parlor table and brought it out here, and put it up on top of this refrigerator!"

"Huh!" Asey said. "What kind of a puddin' was it, anyway?"

"Why d'you ask a foolish thing like that? What *goes* with hard sauce?" Jennie said impatiently.

"In my present state of hunger, I could eat pine-board puddin' with hard sauce," Asey said, "an' enjoy it fine. What I was gettin' at when I asked what kind of puddin'—was it portable?"

"I never heard of a portable puddin'!" Jennie said with a sniff. "Cottage, yes. Portable, no! Why, it was a *plum* puddin', of course, Asey!" As an afterthought, she nonchalantly added, "Square."

"Square what?"

"Just square, that's all! A square-shaped puddin'. It'd been cooked in one of those crazy new glass things. A square-glass steamer."

"A *square* pudding!" Lois gave a little laugh. "Somehow I can't visualize it! Somehow a plum pudding ought to be *round!* What did it *look* like?"

"It looked like a round plum puddin'," Jennie told her, "only it was square! It had a sprig of artificial holly on the top of it, an' it was in the square-glass steamer, just the way it'd been cooked. And I put it up on this refrigerator myself, and I can't see where— what're you laughin' so for, Asey?"

"Just thinkin', if you'd only told me the one thing you had left over from your sale was a *square* plum puddin', I'd have wanted to see it right away. Huh. A square puddin'! It sort of grows on you," Asey said thoughtfully. "If people have started to make square puddin's, the next step ought to be square pies."

"It's probably something that'll creep up on us in the new plastic era," Lois said, and giggled. "Every time you say something's pie-shaped, you'll have to qualify it, and explain in parentheses whether you mean that it's wedge-shaped, like old-fashioned pie, or oblong in the modern manner. Oh, I wish so that I could have seen it! I still can't picture a square plum pudding in my mind's eye—what did it really look like?"

"It looked just as crazy as your old square pies would look!" Jennie answered tartly. "What *I* want to know is, where's it *gone* to? That sprig of holly certainly didn't sprout legs and walk the puddin' out of this kitchen all by itself! Where *is* it?"

"I don't know, but I bet our prowler does," Asey said. "That's why I asked you if it was portable—no prowler or anyone else could've made off very easy with a drippy puddin', or even a half-drippy one. Or an awful gooey one, like that date job you sometimes turn out, Jennie. It'd have to have some substance to get carted off without leavin' a trail, so to speak. Plum in a glass container would be a cinch. An' it fits in with what I was thinkin', too. Person came in here first, swiped it—"

"What *for?*" Jennie interrupted. "What for?"

"Wa-el," Asey said, "I s'pose you might guess he just had an overpowerin' desire to possess a square plum puddin' for his very own. When he heard you an' me comin' down the stairs, he slipped into the shed, an' then when you fainted, he beat it out by the shed door, bearin' the square puddin' in his hot little hand."

He instinctively looked at Lois.

So did Jennie.

"Don't stare at me!" she said. "*I* wasn't your prowler! *I* wasn't in your shed! *I* didn't take it! I never suspected that a square plum pudding *exist*ed! I can't understand why Ann Tinsbury should even *think* of ordering a square plum pudding! The idea never would have entered *my* head, and I've thought up some very interesting and unusual things in my time! Why did she order a *square* one?"

"She didn't," Jennie said promptly. "That is, when I asked her if there was anything she might like to have cooked to order at the cake sale, she said yes, a plum puddin'. She didn't *say* square. It just turned out to *be* square!"

"More important than why she wanted it, square or normal," Asey said, "who made it for her?"

Jennie shrugged.

"Goodness knows! We got lists of things people wanted, and passed the lists around—the club members checked off whatever they was willin' to make and donate. Then they brought the stuff here this mornin'."

"But you wouldn't know which person brought what thing?" Asey asked.

"I can't see that it matters much," Jennie answered. "I remember someone lookin' at the puddin' and sayin' 'Here's a plum!', and I said to put Ann Tinsbury's name on it, it was for her. We were so busy, we didn't have time to go into its squareness much. Why would anyone want to steal it *now?*"

"It opens up some wide an' sort of intriguin' fields of speculation," Asey said. "First thing that occurs to me is that suddenly, someone didn't want it to be here any more."

"I don't like to carp over your choice of words," Lois remarked, "but I don't think that's particularly intriguing. I mean, it's obvious, isn't it?"

Asey grinned.

"I find it kind of excitin'," he said. "Look, from the crack of dawn, that puddin's sittin' here with Ann Tinsbury's name on it. What with all those women millin' around here, anyone could have swiped it any time without arousin' a mite of suspicion. Only no one laid hands on it. In short, as long as Ann Tinsbury was expected to buy that puddin', everythin' was fine. That right?"

"Why, yes, I suppose so."

"Okay. But—Ann Tinsbury is dead. She's never goin' to get her square puddin' now. An' all of a sudden it's terrible important to someone to take that puddin' away from here, even though a child would know there's people here in the house, an' they're runnin' a fine chance of bein' caught an' found out. If Jennie hadn't fainted just when she did, I'd of had 'em by the tail, too."

"But what does it all add up to?" Lois wanted to know.

"That's the intriguin' part," Asey said, "an' somethin' I mean to find out—oh-oh, Jennie! I kind of been waitin' for this! I just seen the sweep of a couple sets of car lights down at the foot of the lane—then they got doused quick at the turn!"

"Hanson, I s'pose. What're you goin' to do?"

"I'm not quite sure," Asey said. "If he's dousin' his lights there, he's probably plannin' to creep up on us like red Indians—offhand, I'd guess that the lobster pot buoy's most likely gone to his head. You got your car keys handy?"

Jennie picked a key ring off a hook by the door, and tossed it at him. "Leavin'? Where you goin'?"

"I think only as far as the shed, at first," Asey said. "I want to find out what's goin' on. See how much you can worm out of him. I'll listen a while."

"What'll we do with *her?*" Jennie nodded toward Lois. "I wonder if she—no, I don't think she'd better stay here with me. She's not very good at dissemblin'. I knew right off she'd been told that old Tinsbury fight business over the phone. You'll just have to take her, Asey."

"But *I* don't want—that is," Asey amended, "I don't think she'd better trail along with me! I—"

"Oh, take her as far as the shed! If you have to rush off, just leave her there," Jennie said.

"Oh, yes, indeed, just leave me *any*where!" Lois added with irony. "In the shed, or maybe you could drop me off in a pond or a swamp or something! Pouf, who cares about Lois?"

"She can stay in the shed. I'll see to her," Jennie said. "Go on, hurry! I want to get your dishes out of the way, an' even if Hanson's walkin' all the way up the lane, you haven't got exactly forever!"

Asey and Lois ducked into the shed as Jennie tied a ruffled apron around her ample figure with the air of a knight donning armor.

The sound of the kitchen door opening abruptly a few minutes later was clearly audible out in the shed.

So was Jennie's snort of indignation.

"Well for *good*ness' sakes, Hanson, how you scared me! Don't you *knock* any more? What's got into you state cops lately, anyway? Only yesterday, one of your troopers slatted out of the Winnicutt Road onto the main highway at ninety miles an hour, an' the only reason he didn't smash me *and* my car to smithereens was that *I'd* seen him comin', mercifully, an' pulled off onto the shoulder—no, no, don't interrupt me! Just you *lis*ten! It's high time someone told you how your precious men *act!* So when he finally slewed to a stop, *I* said—"

Asey leaned back against the shed wall and listened with amusement as Jennie launched into a detailed monologue which he felt sure was sheer improvisation from beginning to end.

She never gave Hanson a chance to slip a word in edgewise, and when she got through, she had him at the disadvantage of being on the defensive.

Furthermore, she airily brushed aside his attempted explanations.

"Don't bother apologizin'! After all, what's done's done! I don't suppose *you* got time to teach manners or courtesy if you haven't got time to *knock* before bargin' into someone's kitchen like an old storm-trooper! For goodness' sakes, what *did* you want?"

Asey grinned.

He knew by the way Hanson started several spluttering retorts that he was well on the way toward losing his temper. Once Jennie succeeded in making him boil over, he'd pour out everything—all he knew, all he'd guessed, and all he was planning.

"I wanted Asey!" Hanson said. "I still want him, too! Don't pretend he isn't here! And don't think you're helping him get away by all this talk, either! I got men stationed outside. I got—"

"Wait a moment, now!"

Asey pricked up his ears. That was the voice of young Dr. Horner!

"Before Hanson gets started, Mrs. Mayo, I want to speak *my* piece! I'm Dr. Cummings' nephew, and of course I've heard all about you and Asey. I want you to know that I disagree entirely with Hanson. I'm against his coming here this way, and I think he's got off on the wrong foot and the wrong track! If he wants to make a fool of himself, that's his affair. But I don't think Asey Mayo had any more to do with this Tinsbury murder than the man in the moon, and I want to go on record at the start as having said so! It's idiotic nonsense!"

At that, Hanson boiled over. In a voice seething with anger, he announced that there were five reasons why he intended to hold Mayo. Asey could picture him ticking them off on his fingers.

First, Hanson said, Mayo was there at the scene of the murder between two and three o'clock, during the time when the girl had been killed.

Second, Mayo had a motive. Hadn't four people already volunteered the information that Asey threatened to kill King Tinsbury or any of his family, if he ever found them in town after that row over Porter patents?

Third, Mayo's lobster pot buoy had been found in the vicinity of the body.

Fourth—and Asey raised his eyebrows at this tidbit of news— one of the girl's curly brown hairs was caught on the rounded end of that same buoy.

"Fifth and finally," Hanson almost shouted, "didn't you just *see* Jameson prove it was her hair caught on it? Well, then, Mayo's buoy was the weapon used!"

"I'm not questioning your expert's opinion," Horner said quietly. "After seeing the evidence he's gathered on your looter with his microscopes and his tweezers and all, I'd never dream of questioning him on anything. I think she was killed by a blow from the buoy. I agree with all your points, but I don't think they *prove* anything at all, least of all Mayo's guilt. If he hadn't told you this was a murder, you'd never have known. To be honest, neither would I. This isn't my line—and he certainly kept me from sticking my neck out! Be reasonable, why in God's name would he have brought the matter up at all, if he actually had killed this girl?"

Hanson said there were at least five more reasons for that.

Mayo was clever, he said. Mayo knew that if the girl were found dead directly after his return, there'd be some talk. So Mayo took the initiative, called it murder. But Mayo had refused to help, hadn't he? And from the start, Mayo had tried to confuse them by lousing up a lot of crazy details.

"He said the girl'd been placed there on the path, didn't he, and to see if we could find any possible weapon near her. All right, so we find the buoy. Why? Because Mayo left it there to confuse us, so we'd ask ourselves if it was there because she was killed there, or if the buoy was a plant. And all that stuff about cod line!" Hanson went on. "Cod line, and a plate of tarts or something! And about him being chased by some guy while he was chasing some other guy! And getting thrown into a mudhole—what's the matter with you?"

"Mean me? I just laughed," Jennie said.

"Well, *I* laughed at that, too! In a pig's eye anyone ever threw Asey Mayo into a mudhole!"

"You certainly can't say he hadn't been *in* one!" Jennie returned.

"Then he jumped in. Probably he's trying to work it up into some sort of an alibi or something. And last of all, Horner, didn't Ann Tinsbury tell her uncle she was going to meet one of the Mayo family? Didn't Kemper Steward say she made some crack about whatever would her father say if he knew who she was going to see?"

"She meant *me*," Jennie said.."She was comin' *here* to the cake sale and lawn fête. And she was comin' to get a square plum puddin' she'd ordered."

"My God," Hanson said, "you're worse than Asey with his miles of cod line and his mudholes! Now look, no more stalling, I want to know—"

"I still think I'd wait if I were you," Horner said. "Physiologically speaking, you're going to be at a bad disadvantage if you meet Mayo in your present overexcited state. You really ought to go home and go to bed, and start in fresh in the morning. Why not—"

"You're as bad as Cummings! That's what he'd say!"

"Good!" Horner returned. "I take that as a compliment. Hanson, I'm not good at ticking reasons off on my fingers, but I still think Asey never would have brought this affair to your attention if he'd killed her. I think that anyone's lobster pot buoy might be anywhere, from what I've seen of your hurricane debris. I think anyone might have picked it up anywhere, used it to kill the girl, and tossed it away anywhere. That old Tinsbury threat angle is just so much tosh!"

"Yeah?"

"It is. You don't kill someone for something that happened thirty-odd years ago. You kill them for something that just happened, or something that will happen very soon, or something that *is* happening right now. While you're busy shooting the breeze—I mean," Horner said quickly, "while you're fiddling around here, Rome is doubtless burning. Your real murderer is probably leisurely leaving town, after having carefully destroyed every shred of evidence against himself, and having had time enough to build up his alibis with concrete, and let 'em harden. In a word, Lootnint, you're just giving this to someone on a silver platter!"

"Oh, the movies!" Hanson said. "That's the trouble with all you people that aren't in this business, you go to the movies too much. So all cops are dumb clucks, and let murderers slip out of their fingers? Yeah! You and Edward G. Robinson both! Jennie, where *is* Asey?"

"Well, Mister Tracy—"

"How's that?" Hanson demanded suspiciously.

"You mean I can call you *Dick?*" Jennie said. "Well, Dick, I'll tell you. Asey's inside the icebox. You open it up, an' he'll put the light on for you! Goodness knows if he's as clever an' diabolical-like as you seem to think, that's the only place he *could* be, an' the only thing he could be doin'!"

"All right, all right, *I'll* find him then! He can't get away. I got men all over the place—all over! Covering the doors, and your car, and his jeep that he'd left down at the end of the lane so carefully, so he could sneak down and make a quick getaway in it—he's *there!*" he said suddenly. "Out in the shed! I heard a noise there!"

"Pooh!" Jennie said. "If you heard anything, you heard the cat!"

"He couldn't be that near," Horner chimed in. "He'd have split his sides laughing long before this, if he'd been listening to you! I *bet* he isn't there!"

The shed door was shoved open quickly, the light was jerked on, and the slim, boyish figure of young Dr. Horner stood outlined against the background of the kitchen.

"He's not here!" Horner looked Asey in the face, winked, and jerked the light off. "I knew he couldn't have been this near—what are those ghastly brown fish speared on that stick, Mrs. Mayo?"

"Hangin' from the rafter? They're smoked herrin'," Jennie said. "You drop by here for breakfast one mornin', an' I'll have some for you. You'll like 'em."

"I wouldn't taste one of the hideous things for love or money!" There was a key pointing at him from Horner's hand, Asey saw, as Horner slowly drew the door to. Making a long stretch, he reached out and took it. "But I'd love to see somebody eat one," he went on. "What d'you take afterwards for a chaser?"

"Asey's somewhere around this house!" Hanson said. "And I'm going to find him. *And* hold him!—no matter what any of you say!"

"All right, let's hunt if you want to," Jennie said agreeably. "I'll take all the jars down from the preserve closet so's you can peek behind 'em, an' we'll sniff at the mothballs under Uncle Ben's Rough Rider suit up in the bottom of the attic trunk. Come along— I'm not goin' to let anyone say *I'm* not co-operative, I'm sure!"

The decisive clump of her footsteps led the others on into the dining room.

"What do we do now?" Lois whispered to Asey. "Weren't you *afraid* when that door opened? I shook!"

"Nope, I know the sound of Hanson's heels—give me your hand, an' watch your step careful. I don't think I better leave you here after all. Hanson might arrest you as an accessory, the way he's feelin'!"

"But where are we going? How can we get out? He said the place was surrounded!"

"I think that talk was all bluff. I know he's shorthanded, an' he's too busy with his hurricane lootin' problems an' such to have many men available—step careful, there's kindlin' all over. Probably there's one outside here, an' one down by where they left the cars. Slow, now. Let me take a peek. You stay right here by the door."

A moment later, he slipped back inside the shed.

"Doggone it, there's two of 'em out in the yard! Huh! Could you maybe dissemble some, d'you think?"

"I dissemble beautifully! I—"

"Not so loud!"

"I'm good! Only I wasn't ever called on before," Lois whispered, "to dissemble after just being told my host was probably a murderer, that's all! The next time, I'll knock you in the aisle!"

"Okay. You're young Dr. Kildare's beautiful pro-tem assistant, then," Asey said. "March out to that pair of cops, an' say Dr. Horner dropped his stethoscope case comin' up the lane an' wants 'em to help you find it. Hunt your way down to the cars, see if there's a cop there, an' get him to help you. Start 'em all back towards here, see, then say you're goin' to have a look inside his car, an' kind of run eager back to it—you want Dr. Cummings's car, mind!"

"I know it."

"Good. Run back to it an' hop in. I'll take you from there."

He could hear Lois chatting brightly with the troopers on the lane as he circled around it, and them, a few minutes later.

Standing well in the shadow of the bushes, he nodded approvingly at her glib explanation to the cop guarding the cars, who frankly didn't see much sense in the stethoscope hunt, and said so.

"Dr. Horner said he'd carried that case through five major engagements and twelve landings, and he certainly wasn't going to lose it now on a Cape Cod lane! Why, it's got a *hole* in it from a Jap bullet!"

"Oh, well, all right. Let's hunt for it, then!"

Asey was waiting at the wheel of Cummings' car when Lois finally dashed down the lane, alone, and threw herself into the front seat.

"That last cop's a toughie," she said breathlessly as the sedan started off, without headlights. "He didn't fall for the case stuff at all. He was right on my heels—how can you *see?*"

"Instinct." Asey's foot bore down on the accelerator. "I wish I'd dared take Junior—but he's so easy to spot! This crate is fallin' apart. Hold on tight, now!"

He swerved off onto the main tarred road, within a few yards made a hairpin turn back on another lane, and then stopped the car.

"What for?" Lois demanded. "What're you stopping here for? Listen—they've already started after us!"

"Uh-huh. I thought most likely they would. We'll see where they go," Asey said, "an' then we'll go the other way. Miss Cook—"

"Oh, call me *Lois!* After *all,* at this point we're practically old—look! Look, there they go now—what're they batting off *that* way at such a clip for? What made 'em pick that direction?"

"They've caught the lights of some other car beyond Snow's house," Asey said. "See the glow there? Huh. They ought to catch up with 'em by the reverse curve, I'd say, an' then they'll buzz all over this section. Then they'll go back for Hanson, an' buzz around all over again some more with him. I guess maybe we'd better stick to back roads for a spell. You hang on tight, because you're goin' to get bounced around good an' plenty!"

"What else happens to me?" Lois inquired. "If I'm caught with you, I mean."

Asey chuckled.

"You'll get twelve dazzlin' offers from Hollywood agents, after the next day's papers, an' twelve mail sacks full of proposals of one sort an' another," he said. "Probably they'll elect you Miss Pin-Up-Accessory-to-the-Fact of the Posthurricane Season. Don't worry. Nothin'll really happen to you at all. I honestly sort of wangled you into comin' along because I wanted you to tell me about Ann Tinsbury."

"Oh," Lois said. "Oh, I see. Like what sort of things?" she added as Asey started up the sedan. "After all, what I knew about her ten years ago at St. Agatha's won't do you much good now, I'm afraid. Ann was eleven, and I was ten—while we were both theoretically past our formative years, quite a bit happened to both of us in the intervening decade—where *are* you going?"

"Just up this lane. Don't get nervous. I knew these lanes by heart before you were born," Asey assured her.

"I never even knew they existed! Look, you *are* going to put on some headlights, aren't you?"

"Shortly. Now, this Tinsbury girl—"

"What does this lane connect with?" Lois asked quickly. "Do you *really* know your way, Asey?"

"Uh-huh. I really do, an' I don't think you really care where this lane goes to, do you? Just stallin' a mite, maybe? Look," Asey said, "Jennie told me an hour ago that your sister Mrs. Peeling an' Ann Tinsbury wasn't very friendly. I'm not askin' you about Ann because of that angle. It's just that I don't know anythin' about the girl at all. Just in a general way, what was she like?"

Lois was silent for a moment. "How well did you know her father?" she asked finally. "I mean, it would be lots easier to explain Ann if you happened to have known him quite well."

"Years ago, when he an' I both worked for old Cap'n Porter, I knew him pretty well," Asey said. "King Tinsbury was really a brilliant sort of feller. Had a mind like a steel trap. When he bit into somethin', he never let go. The only thing I ever underestimated about King was—wa-el, not exactly his honesty, but his lack of scruples, as you might say. He was honest enough in a way. He never denied swipin' those blueprints that caused all that old row. He just never felt any more remorse afterwards than the average man-eatin' tiger'd feel after he'd had a good, satisfyin' meal."

"That sounds like what—" Lois stopped a second, "what a succession of suitors has tried to say about Ann. I don't mean to insinuate that she was man-eating, but she certainly had the faculty for felling the boys with a blow. Even in school she was supposed to be very like her father—brilliant, stubborn, a very loyal friend and an equally devoted enemy. Did you know, by the way, that King Tinsbury disapproved of educating women?"

"No," Asey said. "But I'm not surprised. He had a lot of quirks."

"Quirks is a charitable word," Lois said. "Anyway, King disapproved of higher education for females, but still he gave St. Agatha's a million-dollar plant with simply out-of-this-world plumbing. Dropped in one morning and tossed a check at them, just like that, without even being asked. I suppose he figured that even if he was against Ann's being educated, she might as well be exposed to learning in a place where all the pipes worked. I think you had to be very fond of Ann to understand why she did things. For example, she wouldn't give five cents toward any organized charity, but she worked her fingers to the bone in France—she got a Croix de Guerre, by the way. What I'm trying to get at is that she wasn't as temperamental and eccentric as people liked to say. Neither was her father. In the light of their own reasoning, they were both very consistent. I keep thinking about her ordering that pudding."

"What d'you mean?" Asey asked.

"Well, she never would have broken down and given your cousin Jennie and the rest of the girls a new clubhouse outright, even though the cost wouldn't have been peanuts to her. But," Lois said, "if she'd been amused—or even ordinarily pleased—by that square plum pudding, I can imagine her plunking down a thousand dollars for it without blinking an eye. Just the same, ultimately, as if she'd given part of the clubhouse—only Ann wouldn't have thought so, and she'd have argued your ear off about it being a matter of principle."

"I wonder if Jennie hadn't caught on to that particular quirk in her," Asey said. "The little cherry table was really fixed up with her in mind. Huh. Who's this uncle of hers that Hanson mentioned?"

"That's Kemper Steward. He's King Tinsbury's sister's husband —what's the short way of saying that? I always get mixed up in relations!"

"He's King's brother-in-law," Asey said, "an' Ann's uncle. Simple enough."

"He and Elsie, his wife, were helping Ann settle up the house and things here. Ann was planning to sell the place to some real-estate syndicate, you know. The house itself was a frightful ark of a dump, and I don't know how many hundred acres go with it. Ann wasn't ever a bit dull about business," Lois added. "Her father'd made her handle her own money even back in her St. Agatha days. She never stuck a penny into a chewing-gum machine that she didn't drag out her little account book and dutifully jot it down."

"An' she got along all right with this uncle an' aunt?"

"Very well. She hadn't seen much of them in the last few years, but they were very good friends. Kemper Steward acted as a sort of secretary to King—he was the son of that steamship line Steward, you know. Ripe with money. I mean," Lois said, "if you're brooding about motives, you'd be hard pressed to find any to pin on the Steward family. They're lousy rich, and Ann told me they'd never interfered with her in any way. Never uttered a single word of protest, even though she perfectly well knew they weren't one bit keen on her dashing back to rehabilitate Europe at this particular point—"

"So that's where she was goin' to, after leavin' here? What was she plannin' to do there, anyway?"

"Oh, she had this private relief project for some village she knew very well. Actually, she was sort of obsessed by—I wonder what you would call it? Practical charity, I guess. I remember," Lois said reminiscently, "when she told me about it, I suggested she didn't have to go so far away—that was right after the hurricane, and the whole town was a ghastly mess. I pointed out that just her transportation costs would do a lot of solid good. But she wasn't having any."

"You were here durin' the storm?" Asey said as he detoured carefully around an uprooted tree.

"Ann and I sat it out together. Sister Maggie was marooned in Orleans, and Brian was out helping the other men with boats—can you guess the first thing we saw when we went out of the house in the morning?"

"No. Not after viewin' the inlet beach," Asey said. "I know it could've been anythin' from a flyin' concrete mixer to a stuffed giraffe."

"It was a Mickey Mouse wrist watch!" Lois said. "And, furthermore, it was draped over a branch of the willow tree in our front yard. And still furthermore, it was *going!* Ticking away like crazy! That's one for you to mull over. We couldn't figure it out, whether it blew there, or grew there, or what—"

As she ran on about the watch, it occurred to Asey that Lois was beginning to forget her original statement that she hadn't seen much of Ann Tinsbury. She seemed to have seen Ann and chatted with her quite a bit. She knew Ann's tastes, Ann's family, Ann's future plans.

"So you can't think of any family motives," he said when she paused. "Any rejected suitors around?"

Again, he sensed her faint hesitation before she said no, none.

"Except that Prunn fellow," she added. "The one Maggie calls the leftover refugee. But he's harmless!"

"Left over from what?" Asey asked.

"I never knew exactly what he was," Lois said. "He sort of trickled down here to the Cape with some visiting refugee royalty, and just stayed. He boards with that stern and rockbound character

—Miss Curran—over beyond Ann's. D'you know Miss Curran? She almost might have posed for the Grant Wood picture of the woman and the man with the pitchfork. Both of 'em."

Asey chuckled. "I kept wonderin' this afternoon what was wrong with her eyes," he said, "an' now I know. They got pitchforks in 'em."

"The old gal frankly scares me," Lois said. "I dropped in on her with Ann a few mornings ago to see if her phone might be working—Ann's wasn't—and she practically wouldn't let us in. In fact, she didn't. Stood there at the back door with a bucket of hot water in her hand, all but snarling at us. I wasn't sure she didn't intend to let us have the water right in the face. Ann asked Armand Prunn later how he endured living there, and he said it was very homely. But of course, he's been in any number of concentration camps."

"An' you think he fell for Ann," Asey said, "or for Ann's money?"

"Maggie thought it was Ann, Brian thought it was her money, and me, I wouldn't know," Lois said. "Armand never made a lot of headway with her, anyway, because Ann couldn't understand his lazing around here when there was so much to be done in the world, so to speak. I'll admit he's a beautiful hunk, though. Broad-shouldered. A powerful lad. Maggie always refers to him as Prince Torso."

"So!" Asey let the sedan slow down to a stop. "Powerful, is he? An' he boards over at Miss Curran's, beyond the inlet woods! Well, well! I been hopin' an' hopin' that someone would make some mention of a powerful man who lived around that way! Tell me some more about this big, powerful Prince Torso!"

"I certainly don't think Armand Prunn is any lady-killer in the literal sense," Lois said. "And while I know nothing actually about Ann's love life, I'd guess that her suitors were rejected so hard, they hadn't enough spirit left to take any action against her."

"Did she slap 'em *all* down?" Asey inquired.

"Well—look here, will you remember that I *liked* Ann? We always got along well in spite of—well, we got along! *You* brought

all this up. I never should have. *You're* asking, and I'm merely answering. But Ann did have a rather disconcerting habit of getting
down to dollars and cents. She'd point out what her father had been
making at the age of twenty-eight—or," she hurriedly added,
"whatever age they happened to be."

"How old's this Brian you've mentioned?" Asey started the car
up again.

"Twenty-eight. So is Armand."

Lois ducked neatly out of that trap, Asey thought to himself.

"Anyway," she went on, "practically no one can stand up in a
financial comparison with King Tinsbury, and Ann used to make
that very clear—*do* you happen to know where we are, Asey? I
never guessed there were this many trees left standing on the
Cape!"

"We're about to come onto the main road just beyond the
movies," Asey said. "We've just made a half-circle around the town.
By rights, Hanson ought to have finished the process he always
calls combin' the vicinity, back at my place. Probably he's stormed
back to my house for another look under the beds. An' I'm sure
Jennie an' young Dr. Kildare are thwartin' an' delayin' him all
they can."

"Why d'you call Horner that? I mean, why that scornful tone?"

"I don't mean to be disparagin'," Asey said. "I'm so used to
workin' with his uncle, I suppose I was kind of annoyed to find
this youngster in his place—but I'm feelin' a lot better about him,"
he added. "I've taken back my pooh-poohs. I'm not even goin' to
tell Cummings that the fellow's first move was to look at Ann's
wrist watch, so as to place the time of her death, he said. After all,
as he told Hanson, this line of business is all strange to him."

"What are you planning to do now?" Lois asked.

"I mean to look into the problem of the filched puddin'," Asey
said. "That interests me. An' I'm goin' to find this Prunn fellow,
this Prince Torso of yours, too. If it should turn out that he was
responsible for my mudpack this afternoon, he's goin' to wish he
was back in one of his concentration camps. N'en there's that cod

line. I keep tryin' to put that cod line out of my mind, an' it keeps poppin' right back."

At the intersection of the rut lane and the main tarred road, he waited a moment until a car opposite him, on the continuation of the lane, swung up the steep hill toward the village.

Then he followed.

A moment later, he swerved off the main road so suddenly that Lois lost her balance, pitched forward against the dashboard, and slipped down on the floor.

By the time she picked herself up, the sedan was parked at the far end of the parking lot next to the moving-picture theater.

The motor was cut off, the headlights were out, Asey's elbows were resting on the wheel, and he was whistling softly to himself.

"Why?" Lois asked in aggrieved tones. "I mean, were you trying to break my nose, or did you just want to stun me for a while? Honestly!"

"I'm sorry I had to swoop in here so quick," Asey said. "I didn't have time to warn you. But you see, that car we fell in behind an' was followin' up the hill was Hanson's—"

"He's *that* close?"

"For Hanson," Asey said, "he's red hot. I wasn't payin' any attention to that car when it turned. Hardly noticed it. I never realized whose it was till I seen the fancy seal on the back. Huh! If he's goin' to follow me this close, he's goin' to make things awful sort of awkward. I'm sure he'll drop this crazy notion about me eventually, but until he does, I don't want to meet up with him. He'll only waste time."

"Asey, just what *is* all this about a cod line, anyway?"

From the studied casualness with which Lois asked the question, Asey sensed that she must have been rehearsing it for some time.

"That line? Oh," he said with equal casualness, "it's kind of like the puddin'. Only instead of bein' square an' interestin', it's long an' interestin'."

"But what *about* it? Where *was* it? What's it got to *do* with all this?" Lois persisted.

"It was draped across Ann Tinsbury's shoulders," Asey said, "when I found her. I—doggone it, there goes Hanson past again! I guess we got to sit here a while. When the movie crowd starts comin' an' millin' around, we'll leave on foot. Yup, that cod line's even better material for speculation than the square puddin'."

"D'you mean," Lois said, "that you think it's a *real* clue? Like those cigarette stubs stained with weird shades of lipstick that people are always pouncing on in detective stories—didn't you find any, by the way?"

"Not even one old butt," Asey said. "An' I always wish I *could* find one," he added, "just for the pleasure of conformin' to pattern. An' then I think how plumb foolish I'd look, sniffin' at the butt an' havin' to make some statement like 'This is an obvious blend of burley, latakia, a ripenin' agent composed of various strange fruits, an' just a snack of old rat fur. The lipstick smudge, on the other hand, is very clearly Hauntin' Hope, Shade Variation Number Sixteen.'"

Lois giggled. "'And recently purchased,'" she said. "Don't forget that. Me, *I* couldn't tell old lipstick from new, but book detectives always say it was bought no later than a week ago Wednesday. If butts aren't strewn around in real life, Asey, why are they in most stories, I wonder?"

"Doc Cummings is my detective-story expert," Asey said. "He claims that's the school that always has their villains lie in wait for their victims—"

"You mean *ambush,*" Lois corrected.

"Uh-huh. Doc says apparently the authors can't think of anythin' else for their characters to do durin' a brief pause in the action than to smoke like furnaces. Doc thinks that just like the prohibition gangsters that went to the movies so's to pick up dazzlin' new ideas from mob pictures, murderers today learn quite a lot from stories. They don't often leave fingerprints around much any more—they've even learned to wipe off their trigger-finger print. An' they don't rush off an' leave their victim clutchin' a convenient swatch of Harris tweed in his limply outstretched hand, either."

"I've always wondered deeply about that tweed angle," Lois said. "I mean, I've got a Harris topcoat I had the year before I went to college, and I defy anyone to jerk a swatch of it off in the best of health, let alone in a dying moment. It simply couldn't be done. I always thought it would be more accurate if someone's Harris coat was found with a couple of detached fingernails imbedded in it. They'd certainly give way before the average tweed would. Then there's that perfume, too."

"Which perfume?"

"Why, the haunting odor of some strange exotic Russian perfume, of course!" Lois said. "After finding someone's body, you should notice it at once."

Asey chuckled.

"There was a brisk east wind this afternoon," he said, "an' the smell of the pine woods, an' dryin' leaves. No other scent, as you might say. No, this don't conform to book pattern. In fact, Doc Cummings an' I cling to the notion that if you run into book clues, it mostly only means that someone had access to a lendin' library. They read about the clues somewheres, an' left 'em on purpose to snarl you up. A really smart murderer ought to do the same, usual, common everyday things he always does before he commits his crime—an' the same, usual, common everyday things afterwards, too. A lot of elaborate preparations an' fancy workin' up of alibis isn't bright. For no matter how smart you are in buildin' things up an' weavin' things into intricate nets, like, there's always someone smarter who can tear things down an' pull 'em apart."

"You mean," Lois said thoughtfully, "if you sneak out in the dead of night, after assuring yourself of some intricate and definite alibi, you run more chance of being found out than if you just bopped someone on your way to the post office?"

"Sure. If someone sees you leavin' your house at nine-four, they just think well, well, Lois is goin' to the post office like she always does, an' dismiss you from their minds. But you start tiptoein' around at four in the mornin', wearin' a long gray beard, an' see what you run into. Some day," he added, "ask my cousin Jennie to tell you what happened the night she decided to bury her old rubber reducin' girdle that she didn't want to put into the incinerator because it'd smell so bad burnin'."

"What happened?"

"She found out she couldn't do it. Every time she got it safe underground, someone that had spotted her diggin' went an' dug it up," Asey said. "Her husband an' I laughed so hard we was weak for days. No, I was thinkin' out there in the shed that if I'd planned to kill Ann Tinsbury myself, I'd have done just what this murderer's done. I'd have hit her with some handy blunt instrument that no one could prove I'd had in my possession recent, an' which I can truthfully claim I haven't seen in years. Then I'd put somethin' extraneous an' irrelevant beside the body, like the cod line. Then I'd make a great to-do about snatchin' off some odd object, like the square puddin'."

"Then that cod line really *is* a clue, and whoever put it there killed her?" Lois demanded.

"I don't know if whoever put the cod line there killed her, or whoever killed her put the line there. I've run the gamut tryin' to figure out that fool cod line," Asey said. "But while I was waitin' out in the shed under the herrin', I remembered somethin' that'd be considered awful significant in a book. I remembered a person I'd been watchin' earlier this afternoon, over by the inlet, who'd been walkin' up an' down an' up an' down, the way you do when you're huntin' a certain area for somethin' you've lost. Like for the end of a length of cod line, say."

"Do you know who she is? Did you see her?"

The girl was as breathless, Asey thought, as though she'd just finished a mile run.

And for all the fun she'd been making of book methods, she didn't seem to realize that she had gone and fallen into about the oldest trap of all. She'd let herself be led gently away from the topic at hand until she'd forgotten that she was on guard about it.

He had merely mentioned "a person."

But Lois had said, *"She."*

He said aloud, "She wore slacks like yours, only blue, an' a jacket like yours, only white. I didn't see her close to, but—"

"Asey!" Lois interrupted excitedly, "is that Hanson standing over there? Quick—lean forward so you can see before he turns! I'm sure that was his blue uniform—did you see him?"

"No. I couldn't—"

"I'm sure it was Hanson! I'm going to get out and sneak around and look!"

She was gone before he could stop her.

And he didn't need anyone to ride up on a white horse and tell him that she wasn't coming back, either.

And he certainly didn't intend to walk into Hanson's arms by rushing madly after her.

"So!" he said, leaning back against the car seat. "So she knows somethin' about that confounded cod line, does she? An' what does anyone want to bet me I was describin' the outfit her precious sister Maggie Peeling was wearin' this afternoon? Huh!"

But the time he'd spent with the girl hadn't been wasted. Far from it. While she hadn't presented him with any startling gems of information, she had nevertheless filled in some background for him, he thought. He knew quite a few things about Ann Tinsbury that he never would have found out from Jennie, say. Probably not from anyone else. To be sure, his information was colored by Lois's own brush. That was to be expected. People always colored things in a situation like this. It was instinctive.

But now he had sister Maggie to look into, and possibly even this Brian fellow that she'd mentioned.

And, of course, Prince Torso, the leftover refugee.

If he was the bruiser Lois insinuated—

Something tapped against the car window.

Looking out, he saw an oversized lollypop silhouetted against the glass.

A second later, like a jack-in-the-box, the chunky little girl who'd sold him the hurricane pictures popped up into view.

"Hi!" she said cheerfully. "Did I frighten you?"

"Hi, Mildred. Sort of," he said. "Aren't you out awful late?"

She giggled. "It's only twenty of *eight!* And I'm almost eleven! I'm ten and two months! I'm going to the movies. I thought you'd probably be arrested by now, Mr. Mayo. Mother said you'd be arrested right away and put into *jail!*"

Asey felt his chin go up as if someone had smacked it with a quick uppercut.

"So your mother thinks *I'm* responsible for Ann Tinsbury's death, does she?"

"Oh, sure, everyone does," Mildred said lightly. "They didn't talk about anything else all during supper except you. And everyone kept phoning about it, and all. Most everybody mama knows thinks you did it. Except papa."

"Good for papa! I don't know him," Asey said, "but I'd like to shake his hand. How'd he happen to escape the disease? I mean, what makes him feel different?"

"Papa always feels different. He's an indapennant thinker," Mildred returned, not without pride. "Mother says if he wasn't so indapennant, he'd make lots more money, but papa says he won't be a damn sheep. He says when all the damn sheep stop gossiping, they'll find the snake in the grass is Kemper Steward."

"Ann Tinsbury's uncle?"

"That's right," Mildred said. "I think papa probably knows. Papa was papering up there at Tinsbury's this afternoon when she and Kemper Steward had that fight—that's why papa got mad at Kemper Steward again and walked out. Papa said he wouldn't hang paper for someone that wasn't a gentleman and struck women in the face, and—"

"Whoa up!" Asey said. "You mean Steward hit Ann Tinsbury?"

"That's right, and she hit him right back. And then papa got mad, and then Kemper Steward got mad at papa for interfering, and started to hit *him,* too, only papa wiped the paste brush over his face first." Mildred stopped long enough to giggle. "Papa's always wiping someone's face with the paste brush," she added. "He's really a *very* indapennant sort of man."

"He sure sounds it," Asey said. "Tell me, now, what does this Kemper Steward look like?"

"Why, he's *old!*" Mildred said. "Very old. Older than papa. And very bossy. And he yells at people—that's why papa got mad at him before, a couple of times, because he doesn't like being yelled at. The hurricane blew off the Tinsburys' east roof, you know, and all the upstairs paper had to get done over, and papa says Kemper Steward's lost more wind yelling at him than the hurricane ever had in the first place. He was yelling at Mr. Doane in the drugstore just now when I went in to get this." She waved the lollypop. "He was going to have to wait for his perscription and he was yelling like anything because it would be half an hour. He was stomping and yelling and banging his ole cane on the counter and—"

"Whoa!" Asey interrupted. "Hold it! A black cane? An' is he tall, an' does he have iron-gray hair, an' is he wearin' a gray tweed suit, an'—"

In detail, he described the officious man who'd taken him for a looter over in the inlet woods.

"Oh, you knew what he looks like all the time!" Mildred said.

FIVE

"But I thought you did, really," she went on. "On account of papa said you'd be on Kemper Steward's tail in five minutes, he bet. Papa said he bet you'd tumble to him no matter what all the other sheep were saying—are you going somewheres?" she wound up as Asey stepped out of the sedan.

"Uh-huh. You know, Mildred," Asey said, "I can't exactly claim that you exactly revived my faith in human nature, but you certainly give me a new purpose in life—how many packets of them hurricane postcards have you got left at home?"

"Thirty-one," she told him promptly.

"You bring 'em to my house tomorrow," Asey said. "I've bought the lot. Furthermore, go see," he peered over toward the movie posters, "go see *Hoofbeats of Old Wyoming* an' *Ashes of Passion* on me. An' have half a dozen more lollypops."

Mildred was still standing and staring from him to the dollar bill in her hand as Asey left the parking space by way of the bushes at the rear.

His surreptitious passage through the back yards of Main Street annoyed him. It was a little goading, he thought, to be slinking around your own home town as if you really had murdered someone. He still found it hard to take this Tinsbury business seriously. But you couldn't laugh it off in any airy fashion. Not when it came hurtling at you out of the mouths of babes and sucklings!

"Welcome Home, Asey Mayo!" he muttered as he detoured around the remains of a Victory Garden. "Why in time didn't I *wait* a few days, anyhow? Why'd I have to come bouncin' home so joyous in that tin can? Huh! Stay Away, Hazy Mayo'd be a lot more to the point!"

But he felt better about his circuitous route when he finally peeked in the side window of Doane's Drugstore on the corner.

Kemper Steward was there all right, pacing impatiently up and down in the rear of the store.

And Hanson was there, too, sitting at the fountain and eating sandwiches with Dr. Horner.

They were obviously arguing, and although he couldn't hear a word they said, he guessed that they were still arguing about him, and Ann Tinsbury.

At intervals, Steward stopped his pacing and spoke to them.

It didn't take any master mind to diagnose whose side he was on. He nodded agreement with everything Hanson said, and shook his head violently at everything Horner said. Once or twice he thumped the blackthorn stick on the floor to emphasize his feelings.

Asey watched for a few minutes, and then casually removed the keys from Hanson's car, parked by the side curb, as he made for the mahogany-bodied Porter beachwagon drawn up in front of the store. He knew that vehicle must belong to Steward, even before he saw the name lettered on the door. It had been designed and built exclusively for people like Steward. Bill Porter had even suggested they throw in a set of matched irons or a couple of English setters with every sale.

He ducked down beside the car as the steamed door of the drugstore opened, and then he straightened up when he saw it was Horner.

"Hey, doc!"

Horner swung around.

"I'm over here," Asey said. "Just join me in the shade of the old apple—I mean elm, will you? Your car's in the movie parkin' lot. I'm grateful for the use of it. Is Hanson still—"

"Oh, you can't talk to the man!" Horner said disgustedly. "I've done my best. So has your cousin Jennie, and a couple of others we've run into. But it's no use. I've argued about the fallacies of circumstantial evidence till I'm blue in the face. But these damned little things keep happening to distract him!"

"Like what?"

"Well, Steward's told him that Ann Tinsbury planned to unload a lot of Porter stock, for one thing. Seems she had a lot of it—did you know?"

"I didn't, an' I don't think it matters a whit," Asey said.

"Neither did I. But Hanson feels it does. And then three women who were at your house this afternoon have told him they thought you looked mighty broody—whatever *that* may mean!"

"I probably did," Asey said. "Drivin' all night in Junior's no picnic, an' I was hungry. Anything more substantial like?"

"That expert—what's his name? That laboratory fellow with the microscopes and test tubes?"

"Jameson, you mean?"

"Yes. He claims that the murderer was about your height and build. *I* don't understand how he got it all doped out, I'm sure, but he makes it sound very convincing, and Hanson seems to believe him implicitly."

"Jameson's a smart little man," Asey said. " 'Course, sometimes he does get awful involved about left-handed people dealin' right-handed blows, an' such. An' once he near went berserk because after all his careful calculatin', it turned out that a short woman stood on a two-step stool to stab her husband. But most usually Jameson's inclined to be on the right track."

"I wish you'd get mad!" Horner said with sudden fervor. "You're so damned casual! Hanson isn't kidding—and you're not going to get yourself out of this mess until you've brought him a murderer with a signed confession in his fist!"

"Uh-huh, I know," Asey said. "Hm. Steward's about my height an' build, isn't he? Maybe a bit taller," he added thoughtfully. "Don't think you could maybe sidetrack Hanson onto Steward, do you?"

"Listen, I've even pointed out that *I'm* nearly your height!" Horner said. "And approximately your build, with my overcoat on. I told him I made a call over by the inlet, and got stuck on a road with hurricane trees across it. I've described in detail how I went on, on foot, and got lost, and wandered all over the place. For all *I* know, *I* was somewhere near the girl. I suggested it was just as sensible to hold me as to hold you. In fact, I rather urged him to do just that. I thought it might give you a chance to shake yourself loose—have you given any consideration to the looting angle, by the way?"

"Hanson murmured somethin' about lootin' problems this afternoon," Asey said, "but I didn't pay a lot of attention. You mean we really got looters in what you'd call a menacin' way?"

"We sure have," Horner said. "Uncle was frothing at the mouth about 'em before he left. They'd got into his duck camp on the shore. Seems to be one group that's concentrating on sneaking out valuable antiques from both damaged and undamaged houses—they're hiding their loot somewhere, because as yet no one's spotted it being trucked out. It just evaporates into thin air. Then there's another bunch that's simply swiping anything that's reasonably portable, and of any value at all, from uncle's duck-camp stove to someone's porch swing. Rubber plants, too, I think Hanson said. Anyway, I tried to get Steward to check through Ann Tinsbury's jewelry—it occurred to me that topaz and diamond pin in her coat lapel might have been one of a pair. I've seen pins like that in pairs. Even one would be well worth a looter's trouble—and while it might be a wrench to leave the other behind, it would preclude any nasty suspicion of looting. Don't you think so? If she'd actually owned a pair, people would simply assume that she'd lost one."

"Could be." Asey felt too kindly disposed toward young Dr. Horner to make any cracks, as Cummings surely would have, about the school of advanced if-fing. "What did Steward say to your suggestion?"

"Said he didn't know anything about Ann's gewgaws, and his wife didn't know anything about Ann's gewgaws," Horner answered. "Gave it as his opinion that the type of looter who'd been turning up around here would take everything, including her watch and that money in her pocketbook. Suggested something about writing lawyers about insurance inventories, if Hanson felt interested in Doctor—Um's—speculations. I'm Doctor Um to Mr.

Steward. And Hanson wasn't interested a bit, I might add—look, Asey, what're you planning to do? Can I help any?"

"I don't think so, thanks," Asey said. "I'm afraid you don't know much more about all these folks than I do, an' in a way you've sort of tainted yourself by upholdin' me. I got a kind of miscellaneous assortment of plans on foot, currently involvin' Steward, an' a left-over refugee, an' that confounded cod line, an' a square puddin'."

"Er—a *square* pudding?"

"Wa-el," Asey drawled, "maybe I should've said a square *plum* puddin'. It's more accurate."

Horner stared at him a moment.

"On the whole," he said at last, "I think Jameson made more sense with his calculations about height and build. A square plum pudding, for the love of God! Well, Jennie said if I ran into you, I was to tell you that she had some ideas she was looking into on her own hook. She's taken your jeep, incidentally, and she said that when she got through, she was going to park it where the old ice-house burned down, and wait there in case you wanted her or the car. I trust that the locale means something to you?"

"Uh-huh, I know just exactly where she means," Asey told him, "but if Hanson'd happened to hear her tell you, I'm sure that he wouldn't have."

"I don't doubt it. Since I've been in this town," Horner sounded a little plaintive, "I've heard more that *I* haven't understood! Some of uncle's patients might as well talk Choctaw for all the sense *I've* been able to make out of them!"

"Got thrown by the native dialect, an' our quaint, picturesque characters, huh?" Asey asked.

Horner shook his head. "It isn't that at all—I haven't heard any-one talk the way I expected, the way Cape Cod dialect sounds in books. Oh, I don't mean I thought that everyone would be wearing hip rubber boots and yellow oilskin coats, and carrying spyglasses, and yelling 'Thar she blaows, an' sparm at that!' Everyone's been very decent to me, and I've really understood practically every word they've said—of course, I did have rather a difficult time with quohaug."

"N'en you learned that a quohaug's what a New Yorker calls a clam?"

"More or less," Horner said. "But honestly, I never heard so many understatements in my life! I never heard so much dry humor, and all of it perfectly deadpan, too! I've never seen such damned independence—one old girl of ninety-six threw a bottle of vitamin pills back at me this afternoon! Said no young whipper-snapper was going to tell her *she* had any deficiencies, and if she was deficient in fish oils, why not, who said she was a fish, anyway, she never pretended to be one. Or words to that effect."

"Sounds," Asey said, "like you'd met up with old Aunt Mary Swett. Did she tell you about her life in China?"

"We ran through the Boxer uprising, which she apparently put down with her bare hands, and then she told me just what *I* should eat to put on a little weight. She thinks I'm peaked. Then," Horner said, "then there was a paper hanger in the office last night who practically *dared* me to cure his migraine—d'you know Comrade Rayson?"

Asey chuckled.

"Only by reputation," he said. "I been told he's a very indapennant thinker."

"His thoughts on migraine alone are revolutionary," Horner said. "I never got a chance to tell him mine. Truly, Asey, it's been a very invigorating twenty-four hours I've spent here so far! How uncle stands the pace—say, I think Hanson and Steward are about to come out!"

"Go engage 'em in light conversation," Asey said, "till I get myself stowed away in this beachwagon of Steward's, will you? It's got a Yehudi light, like an icebox, an' I don't want to advertise myself."

Fifteen minutes later, he and the beachwagon were driven into the Tinsbury garage.

Kemper Steward got out, rolled down a garage door, and slammed home a bolt lock. He rattled the door several times afterward as if to assure himself that it was entirely secure.

Then his footsteps crunched away on a gravel path.

Asey tossed off the plaid lap robe he'd draped over himself, and opened the beachwagon door. As the automatic light flashed on, he reached out quickly to press the button in the door frame which would turn the light off at once, before anyone noticed it.

But his forefinger seemed to freeze on the little metal nub.

The garage was wide enough to hold six cars abreast, and long enough to take two cars in each space.

And there was just enough light to enable him to see, hanging from the sides and from the rear wall, more lobster pot buoys than he had ever seen at one time before in all his life.

There were big buoys and little buoys and medium-sized buoys.

There were buoys of all shapes, from single blocks to decorated cylinders.

There were painted buoys and unpainted buoys.

There were buoys in varying states of newness, oldness, and repair.

There were buoys with monograms, with branded initials, with carefully stenciled names, with names that had been painted on any which way, and the *S*'s all backside to. There were buoys with numbers, and buoys with combinations of names and numbers.

Asey stared at them, completely forgetting for the moment the beachwagon's dome light.

They were for the most part local buoys. He recognized almost all of the markings, and knew almost all of the owners. Some of those blocks he had seen hundreds of times out in the channel.

He got out of the car, almost absent-mindedly shut the door, and stood there in the darkness considering the collection.

For it was a collection, of course.

Instead of stamps or butterflies or Indian arrowheads, someone had collected lobster pot buoys. They couldn't have been a legacy from the Callendar family, who hadn't occupied the house in years. Besides, some of the buoys bore names of comparative new-comers to the town.

It must have been one of King Tinsbury's whims, Asey decided. True, the man had lived here only a few months before his death, but if King Tinsbury had wanted a collection of buoys badly enough, and had spread the word around, and had spent enough money, he probably could have achieved this assortment within a few weeks. Aided, of course, by the small fry of the village.

"Now s'pose," he murmured thoughtfully, "that King had one of mine!"

There was no reason why King shouldn't have had one. Plenty of his buoys had been lost. Any energetic child had only to enter his boathouse, for that matter, and swipe one from the pile. And certainly everyone else in the town who had lobster pots was represented in the collection!

"Huh!" he said. "This is broadenin'. Say that Jameson's right. Say it was a buoy of mine that was used to kill the girl. All right. With all of these handy, you certainly don't have to assume, as I been doin' like a fool—an' Hanson, too!—that the murderer necessarily grabbed the thing up from all that flotsam down on the inlet beach!"

On the other hand, he couldn't quite bring himself to think that someone had stolen a buoy from his boathouse, weeks or even days ago, and hoarded it with the girl's murder in mind. Anyone so premeditative wouldn't, he told himself, choose to kill anyone with a quick bash. He'd be the sort who sat at a safe distance behind the telescopic sights of a high-powered rifle.

But anyone could have grabbed a buoy—his buoy—from this collection here. Perhaps someone had coldbloodedly picked out the one bearing his name. Perhaps it had simply been the first one to come to someone's hand.

Kemper Steward could have taken it. Or a looter. Or anyone at all, he thought as he made his way toward the side door.

He hesitated a moment before touching the doorknob.

In an establishment like this, there well might be some sort of alarm system. Hadn't Jennie mentioned King's having dogs, and guards? And Steward had been so very careful about those bolts!

Lightly fingering the outline of the door, he found to his amusement that it wasn't even closed tightly enough to be latched!

He slipped outside, and stood and looked up at the massive bulk of the Tinsbury house.

Jennie's comment flitted back to his mind—that after King's operations on it, the place looked halfway between a cow barn and an old shoe. Sheared of its former columns and balconies, it looked to him more like a reform school, or a jail, or an institution of some sort. There was something stark and bleak about its rigid outlines, and something sinister about the row of massive elms, whose branches, now lopped off, had apparently crashed against the back ell during the hurricane. The trunks were leaning drunkenly and insistently toward the building, as if they were only waiting for another chance to smash it down.

Asey turned up the collar of his coat. Everyone had always laughed merrily about the Callendar balconies and fretwork and all the ornate trim, he remembered as he started to walk slowly toward the place. But at least it had always looked friendly and inviting. Now, if you let yourself listen long enough to the surf crashing hollowly on the shore beyond, or to the moaning of the east wind in those broken branches, you could get cold little shivers running up and down your spine, inviting you to take yourself rapidly somewhere else.

Slowly, keeping in the shadow of the bushes, he walked toward the first-floor window from which a light was glowing.

It was a picture window, a great expanse of plate glass, that faced the garden and the shore. He wondered why it hadn't succumbed to the force of the hurricane, and then realized that there was a protecting shutter above it which could be slid down.

The contrast between the bleak exterior of the house and the bright living room framed by the picture window was so great that Asey found himself wondering if the scene was real, and if he weren't somehow confusing it with some magazine illustration he'd seen for someone's ideal living room of the postwar world.

There was nothing spectacular about it. None of the furniture was lucite or glass brick or gaily colored plastic molded into exotic shapes. The walls were light, the furniture was of light wood, and simple. There were bookcases running along the wall on either side of the fireplace, where a log fire was burning cheerfully. The floor covering was the color of the sea outside on a June day, a cool green-blue. A bowl of dahlias on a table made a splotch of dark red against the wall.

It was the people themselves, he thought, who really gave it the magazine illustration touch—Steward in his well-fitting tweeds, leaning back in a white leather chair, with a drink in his hand, talking to a blonde woman in a housecoat that matched the rug.

They looked exactly like an illustrator's ideal of a middle-aged couple. That was all there was to it.

Anything, Asey decided, from orange juice to life insurance could be sold to an eager public with a picture of the Steward family framed behind that opulent sheet of plate glass.

He would have known the woman anywhere, moreover, as King Tinsbury's sister. She resembled him far more than Ann had. There was that same firmness to her pointed chin, the same high cheekbones, and something about the way she was constantly gesturing with her right hand. King's hands were always in motion.

So, he asked himself, what now?

He could always ring the front-door bell politely, he supposed. He could introduce himself, wangle his way inside like a vacuum-cleaner salesman. He could ask a lot of questions.

In fact, he could probably ask questions till the next major hurricane blew up and finished off what was left of the elms.

And a fat lot of good it would do him, too.

He could guess just how politely and how frigidly he would be brushed off. Even now he'd take odds that they would refer to him as their good man.

His sudden vision of Steward excusing himself during the brush-off made him grin.

He could imagine the whispered phone conversation that would take place with Hanson or one of Hanson's men. He could almost hear the well-bred murmurings of assumed horror with which the Stewards would greet the cops, who would surely rush here and surround the house and grab him in the most approved movie manner.

"Nun-no!" he said. "Nuh-uh! That won't ever work! Wa-el, here goes for the hard way!"

There would certainly be an alarm system inside the house, he thought, as he started to edge his way around to the back. Under the circumstances, after the girl's death, and with the Stewards apparently here alone and without servants, the place would probably be locked up tighter than a couple of proverbial drums, anyway.

But the first rear door whose handle he tried was unlocked, and not closed completely.

Like the garage door, it wasn't ajar. But it wasn't pulled to, either.

It occurred to him as he stepped inside that he would be feeling a lot more comfortable if everything *had* been padlocked, and barred, and barricaded, and guarded by a pack of vicious dogs.

Even one dog would do. He'd settle, Asey thought, for a Pekinese.

Because this just wasn't right!

Things just didn't work out this easy way!

After all, Steward had been so very careful about shutting and bolting that roll-down garage door!

Gingerly, as if he were stepping on eggs, he wove his way through a maze of halls and passages, fully expecting in the next second or with the next step to touch off some wildly clanging alarm.

He didn't.

But by the time he finally found himself standing outside the door of the picture room, the palms of his hands were wet, and the perspiration was rolling down his face in little rivulets.

The first words he heard not only cooled him off in a hurry, but also dispelled the magazine illustration illusion as effectively as if a robot bomb had suddenly landed on the scene.

"It's the paper hanger, Elsie, I wouldn't have an instant's uneasiness if it weren't for that damned paper hanger," Steward was saying. "Except for him, we're perfectly safe! The regular servants have been gone a week, those substitutes of yours from the village know absolutely nothing, no one's been around, nobody suspects anything—except that damned idiot of a paper hanger!"

During the little moment of silence that followed, Asey decided that he was going to like Mildred's papa when he finally met the man.

"Couldn't we—"

"Bribe him?" Steward interrupted her impatiently. "God, no! Don't even consider it, Elsie!"

"But *I* thought—"

"Don't think of it! Promise me," Steward said, "that you won't think of it, or say a word about it, or lift a finger to do anything about it! That would be utterly and completely fatal!"

"But," Elsie persisted, "he's only a paper hanger, after all, Kemper! And you know what King always said—every man has his price!"

"I'll concede that every other paper hanger in the world doubtless has his price," Steward retorted. "I'm sure that any other paper hanger in the world could be packed off on an extended trip to California—but not that idiot Rayson! If you casually dropped a pocketbook full of bearer bonds at that man's feet, and went on your way, he'd only come pattering after you and say that he thought you dropped something, and here it was. It's simply fate that he, of all people, should have been the one to witness that scene between Ann and me this afternoon!"

"Why *did* you fight with her?"

In Asey's estimation, Elsie Steward rated a medal for asking that, the sixty-four-dollar question.

"Oh, she was so damned exasperating!" There was a ring of genuine sincerity in Steward's voice. "I'd held in as long as I could! She had absolutely no business to go messing out of the country again with her refugees and her soup kitchens and all the rest of it! It was time that she sat down and realized her own responsibilities, and took care of her own problems! Ann Tinsbury wasn't any helpless, stupid child. She'd been trained to look after her own affairs, and it was simply her duty to take over King's estate, now, and to manage it!"

"You do say that *so* beautifully, Kemper!"

Asey raised his eyebrows. Was she—yes, that was it! She was insinuating that Steward was acting, merely saying lines!

"Thank you, my dear. Our police lieutenant was properly awed by that speech, too—"

"I still don't see why you told *him* you'd fought with her!"

"I didn't," Steward said smugly. "I simply told him how very badly I felt that I should never have the opportunity to retract my hasty words to Ann during a misunderstanding we'd had just before she left the house for what proved to be the last time. The lieutenant was touched by my honest repentance, and moved by the lovely way I said it. Let me assure you, Elsie, there is no greater advantage than to get your version of a story in first!"

"What d'you mean?"

"I have planted the word 'misunderstanding' in Hanson's mind," Steward said, "before that damned little paper hanger has had a chance to blunder in, as he unquestionably will, and refer to it as a *'fight'!* Hanson, I think, will make tolerant allowances for the difference in terminology. He has already been told about a slight misunderstanding. Now do you see? Hanson," he went on, "was very impressed by my concern over Ann's vast responsibilities— and why shouldn't he be? I was only telling him the blessed, brutal truth! After all, I *did* strike her because she was so very exasperating!"

"There were a few other reasons, too!" Elsie remarked.

"Ah, yes, but I'm sure that neither you nor the police will expect me to go into a lot of selfish detail," Steward returned lightly. "I wanted Ann to stay home and mind her own business, and I shall hardly explain that for purely personal reasons, I violently preferred that Ann, rather than her lawyers, should be running her affairs, and King's, too. I feel—"

The rest of Steward's sentence was drowned out by the thumping of fresh logs being put onto the fire, and the clank of fire tongs against andirons.

But Asey, flattened against the wall outside the door, had heard enough to understand.

Steward had been sticking his fingers into Ann's money, obviously. And he'd figured that he could continue with more safety if he had her to account to, instead of some bunch of hard-boiled attorneys.

Then why in time, Asey asked himself wonderingly, had Steward killed the girl?

Probably Ann, being no fool, had caught on to what he was up to. Little Mildred had reported her papa as saying that Ann had returned Steward's blow. And Lois had remarked that Ann was a fine friend and an even dandier enemy. Probably Ann had found her uncle out, and was preparing to show him up.

And if his guesses came anywhere near the truth, Asey thought, it would have to be rammed home to Hanson with a length or two of rubber hose. Just as Lois had scorned the idea that the Stewards might want or need any more money than they had, so Hanson would point out that the guy was rich already, wasn't he? Well, then!

And there was still one serious flaw in all this, Asey kept telling himself, as Steward continued to bang around with the fire tongs.

By killing the girl, Steward had kept her from disclosing his underhanded activities, whatever they were. But he had also brought about the one situation he had most wanted to avoid— for now the Tinsbury lawyers would take over and run everything!

"The thing for us to do," Steward said, "is to stick to our simple story, and not to permit ourselves to become involved with a lot of romancing. Hanson knows I was around the inlet woods this afternoon. I told him so. But I was there legitimately, with local men, in the interests of the looting problem, and—"

"What's the matter?" Elsie asked as he suddenly broke off.

"I just remembered yelling at a stranger," Steward said. "Fellow running around with a plate in his hand. Gave some name, but I didn't hear what it was—ah, well, I doubt if we'll ever hear of him again. Clearly he didn't know me from Adam. Now you're out of it entirely, Elsie. You weren't feeling well, and you've spent the day lying down. I've driven that home by getting your headache prescription filled in that damn drugstore, and discussing at some length just how you felt and how you bravely suffered. You just never left the house at all."

"Certainly not!" Elsie said. "I never went out. But, Kemper, what's going to happen about the will—"

"Don't say that word! We are not going to discuss that, now, or later, or with anyone! We know nothing about it! Ann's affairs were in her lawyers' hands!"

"But didn't the police ask you who would inherit her money?"

"It was practically Hanson's first question," Steward said. "I told him stiffly that it was really not my affair. I suggested that the bulk of the estate doubtless went to various charities. When it all comes out, we will be dutifully surprised. We will make some very handsome gesture. A new wing on some hospital in her memory, or something like that. Under the circumstances, we can afford to —er—spread ourselves a bit!"

He should have wasted his time and tired his brain thinking about flaws, Asey told himself! Flaws, indeed! The Tinsbury lawyers would be taking everything over and running it, all right, but apparently they would be running it for the sole benefit of the Steward family!

"But," Elsie said, "suppose the lawyers ask us what we know?"

"My dear, they knew Ann. They knew King. And his whims. And hers. We don't have to make any explanations for Ann, or for what Ann should have done, and didn't. We will simply be dazed to discover that Ann made no new will, as she was sharply and repeatedly advised to, and that through a series of extraordinary situations and mischances and what not, the bulk of her estate—which now of course includes King's—reverts to us."

"It really *is* extraordinary, isn't it?" Elsie said slowly.

"Not particularly," Steward answered. "For an otherwise intelligent man, King made rather an unimaginative will. I always wondered in my heart if he thought himself immortal. And, of course, Ann was young. Ann spent the last four years of her life watching people die under the most frightful circumstances, but it never seemed to occur to her that it could happen to her, too. The ramifications of a will that interlocked with King's were far more important to the lawyers than to her. She had forty years more to live, according to the tables. No, we don't need to worry about a thing, Elsie. Except that damned paper hanger!"

"You don't think we should try to shut him up—just," she added hurriedly, "in some *small* way? Couldn't we set him up in a store, or some little business, perhaps? Don't you suppose he longs for a store of his own? King always said people did."

"Regretfully," Steward said, "he doesn't need a store, my dear. If you had troubled to listen to him, you would have learned that skill alone is what counts in his infernal trade, and that he can carry all his tools in his hip pocket. He is also strongly against business, and he particularly dislikes little businesses, and little businessmen."

"What?" Elsie sounded shocked. "He's against *business?*"

"He's anti-business and pro-skill, as far as I could make out," Steward said. "There's quite a dash of William Morris in him. He's also a devout single-taxer and suffers terribly from migraine —his symptoms are very much like yours. We'll simply have to keep our hands off him, Elsie, and let him firmly alone—and hope that Hanson won't choose to take him very seriously. I really feel it's fate that we should be faced in this situation with such an incredibly honest individual!".

"But King *always* said that every man had *his*—" Elsie began.

"Yes, yes, I know. His price. It's also fate, however," Steward said, "that the other person we're faced with is the only person on earth whom King was really unable to buy."

"That Mayo man?"

"Yes," Steward said briefly.

In the silence that followed, something like the point of a razor-sharp knife jabbed itself into Asey's left ankle.

He stifled an involuntary gasp of surprise, and looked down to find a Siamese cat staring up at him with unblinking hatred.

Asey managed to assume what he hoped would be considered a friendly smile.

The cat replied by reaching out a paw in a lightning gesture, and pricking him again.

Something about that unblinking stare promised that on the next attack, he was really going to let himself go—clear to the bone.

Even through it, if possible.

Look, Asey wanted to say aloud, look here, nice kitty! I like cats! Cats like me! Let me tell you about Joe, who lives with us. He's a tiger, and twice your size—not as fine looking as you, to be sure, and maybe you wouldn't like his looks at all. He hasn't got your background, or your personality, or your coloring. But he likes me fine, and I'm sure he'd tell you only the kindest things about me. He'd resent this unnecessarily hostile attitude of yours! Reconsider, boy, reconsider!

Since he couldn't say it, he tried to convey his message by telepathy.

Apparently it worked, for the cat at least stopped staring long enough to blink.

Then Asey realized that he had overdone it.

For the cat, after leisurely rubbing his chin against the scratched ankle, stretched himself up on his hind legs and proceeded to utilize Asey's left leg for a scratching post, lovingly digging in his long claws.

Then he coiled himself, and sprang.

The next second he was on Asey's shoulder, noisily licking his face.

"What's this Mayo like?" Elsie asked curiously.

"I never happened to see him, myself," Steward said. "His pictures always make him out a bit of a hayseed, but bear in mind that that is an absolutely deceptive impression, my dear. If he should tend to impress you as—er—at all haystrewn, remember that the hay is merely camouflage for a steel trap underneath. I've always thought that King came back here just in the hopes of seeing him again. King had an intense admiration for the man. He genuinely liked him. I wonder," he added, "how soon before he'll get around to us."

If, Asey thought, grimly fighting to keep playful paws out of his mouth, and victrola-needle claws out of his eyes, and fur out of his nose, if you'd let this creature get at me sooner, you'd have known me as an intimate friend by now!

He only hoped that he could hang on unsuspected in the hallway until the Steward family had talked themselves out. When he stepped out and faced them—if he had any face left!—he wanted to be in full possession of all the facts. If he had learned nothing else from this eavesdropping, he certainly knew that bluffing would never get him anywhere with Kemper Steward!

"*Us?*" Elsie said. "You don't think he'll really come and bother us, do you?"

"I'm very sure he will."

"But Kemper, what will we *do* with him?"

"Treat him with every courtesy, of course. After all, he's a director of Porter Motors. We'll tell him just what I've told Hanson. We may even permit ourselves to tell him a little more. Yes," Steward said, "with extreme reluctance, I think we shall bring to his attention many interesting sidelights on this tragic situation."

"Whatever do you mean, Kemper?"

Asey was wondering that, too, as he continued to struggle with the cat.

"We'll tell him, for example, that Ann left here this afternoon to meet Lois Cook."

"Oh, did she? I thought," Elsie said, "that she was intending to go to some village affair. A bazaar, or sale, or something of the sort."

"She was. But she was also planning to meet Lois first. She told me so. We won't actually state that as a fact, of course. It might look too much as if we were deliberately trying to attach suspicion to Lois. We'll merely remark that Ann often *did* meet Lois on her way to the post office in the afternoon."

Asey stood very still and let the cat claw away to his heart's content.

"We'll murmur," Steward went on, "how sorry we are that dear Lois has never quite found her proper—shall we say niche? For such a lovely-looking girl, such a pleasant girl, with so many genuine virtues and talents, and with such a charming family—after all, the Cooks *were* quite all right, *I* knew Harry Cook—it's regretful that Lois had to be expelled from *quite* so many schools and colleges. Just mischief, girlish mischief and high spirits, but it does mar the record, rather. Wasn't Lois kicked out of the Wacs, too? Yes, I thought Ann said so. And, of course, we will bring up Brian Lemoyne."

"*Did* Ann love him, d'you think?" Elsie asked. "I've always wondered."

"Certainly Brian loved Ann," Steward said. "He was the only young fellow King ever thoroughly approved of, too. And certainly Lois loved Brian. No question about it. I'm sure she still does."

"That's what *I* thought," Elsie said. "I mean, about Lois. I never really knew what Ann felt."

"Who ever did?" Steward returned. "Anyway, it's a splendid triangle for our Hayseed Sleuth, if he wishes to concern himself with it. And then there's that little refugee fellow who's been underfoot so much—Armand. Yes, we can give Mayo plenty to think about. Just the saga of Maggie Peeling, and King, and Ann should keep him thoroughly occupied for *quite* a long while!"

"When can we leave, Kemper?"

"As the family of the unfortunate girl, we will obviously have to make a lot of grim arrangements," Steward said. "I told Hanson that I was waiting for a call from New York, and that we might have to leave tomorrow if you were well enough, and if we could arrange transportation. Are you so very anxious to get away from here?"

"Oh, you *know* I am, Kemper!"

She sounded as if she really meant that, too, Asey thought.

"I told you," she went on, "how terribly nervous I've felt! And there were more of those noises while you were away. I'm sure there's been someone lurking around. Zanies knew it, too. He was acting so very strangely—it upset me!"

"That cat has a tendency to act very strangely, anyway," Steward remarked. "I shall never forget him the night of the hurricane, my dear. If he'd mounted a broomstick and flown away up the chimney on it, I shouldn't have been at all surprised!"

"He was frightened to death!" Elsie said defensively. "And after all, so were *we*—that awful roof crashing in about our ears! But this was different, Kemper. He wasn't noisy and restless and running around. He simply wouldn't leave my side. He was afraid of someone, it seemed to me. And I'm *pos*itive that I heard someone in the house. This afternoon, and again this evening, and just a little while ago, too!"

"My dear Elsie, however trying they may have been at times, we can be thankful that King's delusions of persecution at least have provided us with an excellent alarm system," Steward said soothingly. "Everything is securely locked. No one could possibly get in here! It's out of the question. Put your mind at rest!"

The cat on Asey's shoulders suddenly became very still.

Then its body began to tremble.

But Asey's slightly frantic attempts to set the animal down

on the floor were met with the most savagely intense battle.

Nothing was apparently going to dislodge Zanies from what he considered a safe and friendly haven.

After briefly estimating the extent to which those long claws were dug into his coat and beyond into his shoulder, Asey decided to give up. Unless he had assistance, those claws couldn't be pried out without hurting the animal.

Cat or no cat, he would simply have to stand there quietly.

At any rate, he thought, it was now reasonably clear that Elsie Steward was right, and that her husband was very wrong.

Someone had been around the house, someone had monkeyed with the alarm.

That explained why he had found the garage door and that back door open.

That was why he hadn't run into any of the troubles he'd expected.

Where, he asked himself, was this person now?

If the Siamese was any gauge of the situation, the person couldn't be much more than ten feet away at this very moment!

And there wasn't much that he, personally, could do about it.

Acting as a foxhole for ten pounds of frightened, steel-muscled, barb-clawed cat, Asey decided, was just about the equivalent of a strait jacket.

While he theoretically had more freedom of movement, a strait jacket wouldn't be lined with the little razor blades now biting into his shoulder and his neck every time he took a breath!

"Who *do* you think killed her, Kemper?" Elsie said suddenly.

"My dear, *I* don't know!"

Asey felt his jaw drop.

Steward wasn't acting. That wasn't a stage line!

The man had spoken the truth, and Asey knew it. Sometimes, he thought, you couldn't be mistaken!

"I can't think," Steward went on heavily. "I honestly can't think of anyone who would actually profit by her death. Except us. I honestly can't imagine who could have wanted to kill her. If only she had been robbed, I might be able to understand it. Otherwise, I can only think that it was all some frightful mistake—by the way, d'you happen to remember a topaz and diamond flower pin of Ann's?"

"Yes, indeed," Elsie said. "You mean that pair she often wore on her coat lapels?"

"A *pair?*"

If Steward hadn't asked that, Asey thought, he would have, himself.

"Yes. Brian gave them to her—oh, years ago. When they first met. She was always very fond of those pins. Why do you ask about them, Kemper?"

"Because Dr. Horner asked me about them, apropos of his theory that some looter was responsible for killing her. I'm afraid," Steward said, "that I rather snapped back at his suggestion. I said that only a very idiotic looter would take one pin—I didn't know it was one of a pair, actually, you know I never notice that sort of thing—and leave behind another pin, and her watch, and her money. But now that I've had time to think it over, I'm not so sure he may not be on the right track. Some of the thievery has been very selective—it was a smart looter who took only those first editions from Logan's."

"Then you don't think Mayo killed her?" Elsie asked. "Didn't you ever?"

"No, never, not for a moment. I can think of no earthly reason why he should have. Of course, Hanson and the natives are all excited over some old threat Mayo made against King, years ago, and it certainly would be very foolish of me to dissuade them from any such thoughts. But," Steward said, "the cold fact remains that you and I profit, my dear. And no one else does!"

"You never liked her, did you, Kemper?"

"Ann? No. No," Steward said, "she never let anyone get close enough to her to like her, or dislike her. You know that yourself. You've tried since she was a little child, since her mother died, but you couldn't scratch the surface!"

"But she was generous, and charitable—"

"She was very generous, and very charitable," Steward interrupted. "I always said so. She gave things very freely, in her way. She worked very hard at it. But I know less about her than I know about that damned paper hanger. And I feel less!"

"Really, Kemper!"

"When Hanson led me to her this afternoon, I thought of all the things I ought to be feeling," Steward said, "and wasn't. I was sorry, desperately sorry for her, and that was absolutely all. I wasn't sorry about those bonds of hers. I didn't feel any regret for what I'd done. I still don't—what? Oh, not now. That will all be smoothed over now. But Ann could have helped me when I asked her to. You know that King would have. He would have understood. Ann didn't, or didn't choose to. I suppose if her being the way she was could be blamed on anyone, the fault was King's entirely. He—"

The cat suddenly tore his claws from Asey's shoulders, leapt to the floor, and scuttled into the living room as if he were being pursued by a pack of large and very hungry dogs.

"Zanies!" Elsie said. "Come here, darling—see, Kemper, look at the poor lamb! He's frightened again! He's simply trembling like a leaf! Come, Zanies, come here—Kemper, something's awfully wrong! Do go put on some lights and take a look around, please! You can't look at this cat and tell me that everything's perfectly all right! I know it isn't!"

As he heard Steward's approaching footsteps, Asey ducked from where he had been standing, outside the living-room doorway, into a long hall.

Then, as a thousand lights seemed to flash on all at once, he slipped into the first open doorway that was at hand.

Before Steward had snapped on those lights, Asey's eyes had been accustomed to the darkness. But now he couldn't distinguish anything in the room in which he found himself. He had no sense of its shape, or its size, or the location of its furniture.

There was no longer any reason for him to avoid Steward, he

thought as he put out a groping hand. Except that if he announced his presence to Steward, he would also announce it to this mysterious intruder. Perhaps, if Steward ran into the fellow, he might be glad of some unexpected help.

His hand touched a table, and moved onto the back of a chair. As he started to take a tentative step away from the vicinity of the doorway, he was grabbed, and once again picked up like a baby.

"Steward!" he yelled at the top of his lungs. "In here! *Here!*"

This time, he thought, he wasn't going to be tossed around like a beanbag.

This time, things were going to be different.

And they were, too.

By the time Steward snapped on the lights of the room, Asey and the iron-muscled intruder were having it out in the center of the floor.

This time *was* different!

This time, someone else was going to get tossed around, Asey thought with satisfaction!

And probably someone else would have, too, if Steward hadn't swung his blackthorn stick at just the wrong moment.

SIX

ASEY waked up in the middle of a field of daisies with a bright noonday sun shining down in his eyes.

Then young Dr. Horner's face blotted out the sun, and Asey closed his eyes and told himself he knew it had been a chandelier, all along, and that the field of daisies was a white polar bear rug. He could feel the fur against the back of his hand.

Then the fur began to lick his fingers.

"Zanies!" Elsie Steward said. "Zanies, do come away from him! Come here, Zanies! I can't understand it. He simply hasn't left Mr. Mayo's side, do you realize that, Kemper? Ordinarily he doesn't like strangers at all. Particularly strange men. He thinks they're all veterinarians," she added, "ever since he had that tooth pulled. Zanies, stop bothering him!"

Zanies ignored her.

"Well, doc, what about it?" Hanson's voice sounded oddly brisk. "How is he? How's he coming? *I* thought he blinked just then."

"He's all right!" Horner said. "He's all right, as I've told you some seventy thousand times before! He's coming out of it, he's perfectly all right!"

"Looks terrible to me!" Hanson said.

"You wouldn't look any better, chum, if you'd been belted with a blackthorn stick—listen, can't you stop hovering and fretting for just a minute?" Horner demanded. "I'll admit I have no control over this cat. He's made up his mind to hover and fret, and that's that. But you are in the way, if you don't mind my saying so. Go pick up the rest of the baubles! Go on, Hanson. Go hunt up some more diamonds!"

"We got 'em all."

"Well, pop outdoors and hunt up the fellows, then. Go search—"

"My boys are scouring—"

"Oh, that word again!" Horner said. "I wish you'd stop saying it! Can't you ever do anything but *scour,* for the love of God? Can't you break down and actually *find* somebody once in a while? All evening long you've been scouring around for Asey, and he had to catch a haymaker before you caught up with him! Go on, Hanson, go out and find the nice looter!"

"Look, we got here as fast as we could, didn't we?" Hanson said. "We came as soon as Steward got hold of us! But this guy had a head start, didn't he? Well, the boys are doing all they can do, and as well as they can—hey, doc, he's opening his eyes! Hey, Asey, you all right? How you feel?"

"Fine," Asey said. "Dandy. Just dandy. Never felt better in my —ooop!"

Zanies had jumped up on him, and was starting to lick his face.

"Really!" Elsie Steward said delightedly. "I think this is the most amazing thing! Kemper, are you watching this? Isn't this the most perfectly amazing thing you ever knew?"

"Frankly," Steward said, "I think it's a lot more amazing that the total contents of your jewel box, and Ann's too, are intact. I find that considerably more amazing than Zanies' sudden passion for Mayo here—"

"No more of that, now!" Hanson said sharply.

"Er—no more of what?" Steward asked.

"You know! I told you! Mayo didn't have anything to do with your old diamonds, and don't," Hanson said menacingly, "don't you go insinuating that he did, see? I won't have any more of it!"

"I didn't—" Steward began.

"Don't!" Hanson interrupted crisply. "Doc, can't you get that cat off him?"

"If you want to try, I've got plenty of iodine in my bag," Horner said. "I'm not touching him. I've learned my lesson! Asey, Zanies won't move for anyone, but perhaps if you gently told him that you preferred him on the floor beside you—"

"Zanies," Asey said, "sit down beside me, there's a good cat."
Zanies promptly obeyed.

"I never saw anything like it! It's simply amazing! But," Elsie Steward added casually, "it was all insured, wasn't it, Kemper?"

"The jewelry?" Steward had no difficulty in picking up her conversational thread. "Yes, of course. We shouldn't have lost—"

"I don't want any more talk about it!" Hanson said. "Not another word! I mean it! Asey, how do you really *feel?* Are you all right?"

"Sure, I'm feelin' better," Asey said. "I don't know as I got any overpowerin' desire to play first base for the Dodgers right away, but I'm recoverin'. What happened, anyway?"

"Your friend—" Steward said, but Hanson wouldn't permit him to continue.

"There you go again! Now, listen to me—whoever he was, he wasn't Asey's friend, see? Once and for all, don't you say again that Asey had anything to do with this jewel thief, or looter, or whatever you want to call him! You hear me?"

"I hear you," Steward said, "and I'm sure people in the village managed to catch every word, too."

"You know what Steward here thought, Asey?" Hanson gave no indication of knowing that he had just been slightly rebuked. "He thought you and the jewel thief were in cahoots! He had the nerve to call me and say he'd got one of the thieves—meaning *you!* Can you beat that? Can you tie that one?"

Asey looked at Horner, who was biting his lip, and at Steward, who was very red in the face, and at Elsie Steward, smiling at him pleasantly.

Then he looked up at Hanson, scowling with honest indignation.

"Wa-el," he said, "maybe Mr. Steward didn't know me, that's all."

"He recognized you! He knew who you were! And he *still* thought." Hanson paused to shake his head in disbelief. "I can't get over it! He still thought *you* were a thief!"

"May I point out," Steward said in restrained tones, "that *you*

told *me* that he was a murderer? Under the circumstances, I quite
fail to see why there should be all this rather melodramatic to-do
merely because I referred to him, whether inadvertently or otherwise hardly matters, as one of the looters!"

"Listen, I know Asey!" Hanson said. "He might maybe kill
someone—though I never actually *called* him a murderer, see? But
—he wouldn't *steal!*"

"My dear good man," Steward returned, "there on the table are
two jewel cases whose contents you have had a chance to see, yourself. I came into this room, turned on the lights, and there were
the cases on the floor, and there was Mayo—"

"Fighting your thief for you, wasn't he?" Hanson demanded.
"Well!"

"When one finds two quite strange men in one's house, apparently engaged in a struggle to the death," Steward said, "with
two full jewel cases in the offing, one does not immediately jump
to the conclusion that the man in the black sweater is a bad man,
or villain, while the man in the duck coat is a good man, or hero,
valiantly battling to save one's property!"

"That's fair enough, Hanson," Asey said quickly. "After all,
Mr. Steward barged in here an' found that fellow an' me fightin'
tooth an' nail, with the loot right out in plain sight!"

"But he knew you, didn't he? Sure he did!" Hanson said. "He
knew who you were, all right. And if he saw you fighting somebody, he certainly ought to of been able to guess what was going
on! Anybody could of figured it out from there! It isn't like he'd
found you and this other guy with each of you holding a jewel
case under your arm, and both of you holding hands and cooing
at each other like doves!"

"My dear Hanson," Steward said wearily, "just a few hours ago,
you were far less benevolently disposed toward Mayo, and far from
convinced of his sterling worth as a champion of law, order, and
justice. Please don't lose sight of that fact, and please do try to be
reasonable! I found your murderer fighting what seemed to be a
fellow thug, with my family's jewels at hand. I drew the obvious

conclusion, that the two of them—please do let me finish, will you? I naturally concluded that the two of them had robbed us, and were engaged in a violent quarrel over the spoils!"

"Listen!" Hanson raised his voice. "Listen here, Mr. Steward—"

"*You*," Steward outshouted him, "you listen to *me*, Lieutenant Hanson!"

"Kemper, dear, really!" Elsie Steward said. "Must you yell so?"

"Apparently I must, if I wish to be heard! I will not be screamed at, Hanson! I refuse to be scolded like a little child for drawing quite obvious conclusions from the scene which I interrupted. Is that quite clear? Good! Now," Steward went on, "I'll be very honest with you. I did not feel, this afternoon, that you were being very intelligent or very logical in swallowing whole that old legend of Mayo's fight with King Tinsbury, and his threat, and so on. I did not think that Mayo killed Ann—"

"Whyn't you say so, then?" Hanson interrupted. "Why didn't you?"

"You were so very, very positive!" Steward said quietly. "If you will only think back, my dear fellow, if you will only think back! I didn't agree with you, but after all, this sort of thing is your business and your life work. It's not mine. I never pretended to know the first thing about the intricacies of crime detection. The point I wish to make is that while I did not think that Mayo had anything to do with all this, originally, I am now far less sure."

As Steward paused, Asey looked up at him thoughtfully and wondered what the man was getting at.

Hanson, bristling a little, asked him. "What d'you mean, anyway?"

"I have been remembering some things," Steward said, "which I considered unimportant. I saw Mayo this afternoon on the shore at the edge of the inlet woods—not very long after Ann left the house. And I'm very sure now that he is the man I chased later—I followed him clear to the marsh, where I lost all trace of him."

"So," Asey said, "so you were the other slice of bread in that sandwich! Huh! It's nice to have some of that cleared up."

"So it was you!" Steward said. "You admit it?"

"Look here, if you saw him in the woods, and then again later," Hanson said, "whyn't you tell me so before this? What was the idea? What were you keeping it such a secret for?"

"I wasn't. I simply didn't know then who he was," Steward answered promptly. "I didn't know him!"

"Oh, come now! I told you!" Asey didn't particularly care whether Steward had recognized him or not, but this seemed an excellent place to apply a spot check to all the things Steward had said in general. And he clearly remembered Steward telling his wife, back there in the living room, that he hadn't heard what name the stranger gave. "When you asked me for some sort of identification, I told you my name was Mayo. Don't you remember that?"

"But you weren't wearing the clothes I have always associated in my mind with Asey Mayo!" Steward said without hesitation. "As a matter of fact, I actually didn't hear what you said your name was. Later, when I chased after you—"

"Why didn't you tell me about this before?" Hanson interrupted.

"I didn't think it mattered any! He wasn't wearing the clothes I associate—"

"Look, if he was stark naked, and you saw him or anyone else around the woods there at the time she was killed, you'd ought to have spoken up and told me so!" Hanson said. "If you chased some suspicious person later, you'd ought to have told me all about that, too. Anyone that was around there matters! Whyn't you mention any of this to me before? What's the idea? Are you trying to keep things back, huh?"

"Not at all! I—"

"Or," Hanson went on, "are you just making this up as you go along?"

"I'm telling you the simple truth!" Steward protested. "Just the simple truth, that's all!"

"Yeah? You told me that you were around those inlet woods

this afternoon," Hanson said, "but you gave me to understand the simple truth was that you were with some of the men from the town, looking into the looting problem. You never said the simple truth was that you were wandering around those woods by yourself! Now what I'd like to know is, which simple truth is true?"

"Why, I—er—I—"

Steward finally hesitated.

Asey looked up at Horner quickly, and saw that the doctor had noticed, too.

So had Elsie Steward. But she wasn't looking nervously at her husband, or biting her underlip, or tearing her handkerchief to shreds. She just leaned against the arm of a chair, and watched the cat.

"Why, I—er—" Steward said again.

"I thought so!" Hanson said with triumph. "I thought so! Can't quite make up your mind if what you said first was true, and you were with the men all the time, or if all this stuff about seeing Asey all over the place is true, in which case you got some explaining to do, yourself!"

Steward was in an awkward position, Asey thought to himself.

After so carefully planning just what he was going to say, and just how much of the truth he intended to divulge, and just how he was going to color it, Steward was now slightly hoist with his own petard. Although these additional entries of his were the plain and simple truth, they none the less sounded odd when superimposed on his original version of the truth.

Smarter people than Steward had got themselves into just the same jam. But Steward's face looked as if the end of the world was advancing rapidly up the gravel driveway outside.

"All your talk about that misunderstanding you had with the girl," Hanson went on. "Simple truth of that wouldn't be that you'd had a *fight* with her, would it? Suppose you just run over that part of the simple truth again for me, right now!"

Steward ran through it glibly enough.

"In short," he concluded, "I felt that Ann's duty was to stay home in this country, and look after her own affairs!"

"Okay," Hanson said. "Then what did you do after she left? What time did you leave here? When did you meet the men down at the inlet beach? When did you meet Asey by the woods—if you did! What happened then? When did you chase Asey—if you did! Let's us get our teeth right into this, Mr. Steward!"

Steward went through Hanson's questions one by one, naming the names of the men he'd been with, and earnestly attempting to give the approximate time of his every movement.

Asey thought he couldn't have done much better if he had been on the witness stand.

But Hanson wasn't satisfied, and he said so.

"Up to the time you started to try and throw suspicion at Asey," he said, "you sounded pretty good to me. That was a good, honest-sounding story you had!"

"I repeat, I've told you the simple truth," Steward said. "I didn't think to tell you about meeting Mayo because until I saw him here in his—er—more publicized clothes, I honestly didn't realize that he was the man I'd seen this afternoon. As for my chasing after him, he was only one of half a dozen we chased. I didn't think anything of it—until I realized that the man I'd chased to the marsh was also the same man I'd spoken to earlier, and that the man I'd spoken to earlier was Mayo! You know very well that after the petty thievery that's been going on here recently, it's almost automatic to chase anyone who's running—we've recovered a number of small items that way. But I've been perfectly honest with you, I assure you, Lieutenant Hanson!"

"Well," Hanson said with a touch of irony, "now I'll be perfectly honest with you, Mr. Steward! I never gave you a moment's thought this afternoon. But now that I've thought you over, I've come to about the same conclusion you've reached about Asey. I'm a whole lot less sure about you!"

"May I ask why?"

"The minute I looked at the outside of this place here," Hanson said, "something seemed to strike me. I begun to wonder about you."

Asey smiled. He knew exactly what Hanson meant.

"And then," Hanson said, "I saw all those lobster pot buoys out in your garage, while my men and I were hunting around for the guy that got away. Couldn't have had a buoy with Mayo's name on it, could you? And maybe it's also the simple truth that the bulk of the Tinsbury girl's estate doesn't go entirely to charity, huh?"

"You mean," Steward said with a sigh of resignation, "that you are now putting me in the place—er—formerly occupied by Mayo? Is that it?"

"I mean that there certainly seems to be plenty of things," Hanson said, "that you and I are going to go into!"

"Before you start," Asey said as he got to his feet, "let me get straightened out on the story of what happened, will you? I was mixin' it up with that fellow, an' Steward waved his blackthorn stick at the place where my head happened to be at the time—an' then what?"

Steward raised his right hand, and Asey noticed for the first time that it was bandaged.

"He went for me," he said, "in a sort of flying tackle. I would have sworn that I was going to crack his skull with my stick, but somehow—er—"

"I know," Asey said sympathetically. "When he an' I first got together this afternoon, I would've sworn I was goin' to wrap him around his own neck like a scarf. I ended up in a mudhole."

"As I went down, my hand caught the glass lamp," Steward pointed to the shattered fragments which had been brushed into a corner of the room, "and I cut myself rather badly. He went dashing out into the hall past Elsie, leaving the jewel cases behind. I will have to admit that I didn't recognize you," he added, "until Elsie was bandaging me up a few minutes later. Then I called Hanson, and asked him to bring along the doctor. The rest I believe you know."

"Couldn't have been the simple truth that you really *meant* to crack Asey's skull—" Hanson began.

"Hold it," Asey said. "I want to know what that fellow looked like. I was a little too busy to notice him much in the split second between the light goin' on an' me goin' out like one. Will you describe him for me, Mr. Steward?"

"He was wearing a black sweater," Steward said, "and he was dark. Dark hair. And quite tanned."

"But what did he *look* like?" Asey persisted.

"I'm afraid that's all I can tell you," Steward said. "I should know him if I saw him again, of course, but I can't add any more detail."

"Mrs. Steward," Asey said, "did you notice him at all?"

"Oh, I just had the merest glimpse of him, really," she said, "as he went rushing past me in the hall on his way to the front door. He was no one I'd ever seen before—around here, or anywhere else. He was quite tall—about your height, Mr. Mayo, perhaps even a little taller. Not stocky, but still rather muscular and burly looking. He wore dark trousers—Kemper, dear, what's that suit of yours I always liked so much? We gave it away to the Russians —or was it the Poles?—last winter."

"Covert," Steward said.

"Dark gray *covert* trousers," Elsie said. "I've been trying to re-member the name of that material. Almost black. And he wore a black sweater with a round neck. And I think no shirt underneath. His face," she paused and frowned, "well, it wasn't really what one thinks of as thuggish, if you know what I mean. His eyebrows were rather heavy, and his nose was rather aquiline. I don't quite know how to describe it, but he ran—well there was an elasticity to the way he moved. A co-ordination. I think he was probably around twenty-six or twenty-eight. I do wish I could tell you more," she concluded. "But of course I didn't really get a very good look at him."

Horner coughed, and avoided Asey's eyes.

"I think," Asey said, "that we'll know him if we see him again.

Thank you. Hanson, that fellow's your real professional looter, I think. I'm sure he's the fellow I ran into in the woods this afternoon, the one that led me such a chase. First he cracked branches to let me know he was there, an' then he led me on an' on. I think I understand why, now."

Hanson said he was sure that *he* didn't understand any of it.

"Remember bootleggin' days?" Asey asked. "I wonder if someone isn't maybe tryin' to hijack this fellow, an' he knows it, an' is on guard. Or else he sensibly realizes he's very easy pickin's for a good hijacker, an' is on his guard anyway. Seein' me in my city clothes, I'll wager he thought I was someone he knew. Or else he wanted to get a good close-up look at me. I can't think of any other reasons for his leadin' me on. An' then when he found out I wasn't who he thought, or anyone he knew, he let me go—if you could call it that."

He leaned back against the black marble mantel, and thought about Ann's topaz pin that had been one of a pair. He wanted to bring that up, but he didn't want the Stewards to know quite yet that he had heard their conversation. He was going to save the gleanings of his eavesdropping to use as a weapon when someone —either Hanson or Steward—finally got around to the question he'd been waiting for.

He shifted his position against the mantel—when Zanies used his claws, he put his soul into the gesture, and the scratches on his shoulders were far more painful, Asey decided, than the aftermath of that more spectacular crack on the head. One small gash on his collarbone was particularly annoying. It seemed to bite him every time he moved.

"I wish," Horner said suddenly, "that you'd stop swaying gently, and sit down, Asey!"

"I'm all right," Asey said with perfect honesty. "I'm fine. Only thing—"

"You're going home and go beddy-bye, you know," Horner interrupted, "just in case you happen to be harboring any mad thoughts about staggering around and detecting—no, don't protest! This is *my* department! I'm going to put you to bed. And have Jennie stand guard over you with a rolling pin. You took the hell of a wallop, and you needn't think you're going to do any more dashing around tonight. You're not!"

Asey grinned.

"I mean it!" Horner said.

"I'd sort of forgot, doc," Asey said gently, "that you was so awful young! Your uncle'd know better than to tell me anythin' like that. An' after all," he shot a quick look at Hanson, "I can't do much of anythin' anyway till I find out whether or not I'm bein'—uh—held for future reference. There isn't a mite less evidence against me now than there was. In fact, there's a mite more, if you add Mr. Steward's verification of my bein' so near the scene of the crime this afternoon!"

"Oh, Kemper didn't mean to insinuate anything like that, I'm sure!" Elsie said. "Look at the way Zanies has taken to him, Kemper! You certainly can't think of him as—er—really, I know he doesn't, Mr. Mayo!"

"I do dislike to appear so crass and so stubborn in this universal and widespread reversal of feeling in regard to Mr. Mayo, my dear," Steward said blandly. "It's very reactionary of me, I'm sure. But there remains, after all, one rather important question which has not been thoroughly explained."

Asey grinned.

It was finally coming.

"What's that?" Hanson demanded. "What question?"

"Exactly what was Mr. Mayo doing here in this house, if he didn't come with the looter?" Steward returned. "Either Mayo came with him, or he didn't. You seem to feel it's impossible for Mayo to have any connection whatsoever with this fellow, and of course, it's quite possible that you may be right. I dare say you are. But it hasn't been explained to me what he was doing here—if he came by himself!"

"I was listenin'," Asey said quickly, before Hanson had a chance to speak.

"*What?* What's that?"

Steward didn't merely look surprised and bewildered, he looked aghast.

"Listenin'. An' I'm sure," Asey said, "if I'd stood over you an' cracked a whip, I couldn't possibly have found out a bit more than I did. As you pointed out, you seem to be about the only people who really stand to profit any by Ann Tinsbury's death."

He presented himself with a little mental pat on the back for having held in until now about his eavesdropping.

There wasn't, he thought with a certain amount of relief, going to be any more loose talk from Kemper Steward on the topic of what he had been doing, creeping around King Tinsbury's house!

There wasn't going to be any belligerent backtalk from Hanson, either, although he had a bona fide charge of breaking and entering in the nighttime, if he had happened to want to take full advantage of it.

Steward was far too disturbed to attempt any further attacks or insinuations.

And Hanson was apparently far too interested in what was going on to consider bothering with the breaking and entering issue. Asey rather even doubted if its possibilities had occurred to him.

"*Listening?*" Steward sounded as if he still couldn't believe the testimony of his own ears. "You were listening to me? To Elsie and me? To us? In the living room? You *heard?*"

Asey nodded.

Almost unconsciously, he suddenly moved from where he had been standing by the fireplace to the center of the room, under the chandelier.

And just as unconsciously, Hanson moved aside for him.

Young Dr. Horner, after a swift look around, decided that he was the only person there who grasped the significance of that small shift in position.

It was his firm impression that Asey had just taken over command of this business, lock, stock, and barrel.

"If—if you heard that conversation in the living room," Steward paused and moistened his lips, "then you know the truth."

"Uh-huh," Asey said. "After a fashion. I heard the truth—Zanies, you leave my ankles alone! No, you can't jump up on me, either! I heard the truth as it'd be spoken by someone who seemed pretty sure he was goin' to get accused of murder, sooner or later. I know your openin' gambit, as you might say. I know your future propaganda plans—an' you know now that you made a real bad tactical error in figurin' you could connect me up with your jewel thief, an' so make me out even more of a criminal than Hanson ever dreamed I was. You didn't succeed in pilin' a little crime onto a big one an' makin' everythin' look more awful. You just made it a little silly for anyone to think of me as a nasty criminal at all. Didn't you?"

"You heard the truth!"

"An' by tryin' to locate me more accurate-like, in the inlet woods this afternoon," Asey went on, "you've gone an' placed yourself more accurate, haven't you? Uh-huh, I understand your policy of insinuatin' suspicion around, all right, after listenin' to you. An' I hope you understand now just how hard that sort of thing can backfire!"

"I tell you, you heard the truth!" Steward repeated stubbornly.

"Could be, I s'pose." Asey's voice had a purring note which Hanson recognized and pricked up his ears at, and which caused Zanies to look up at him with renewed admiration. "Could be. Only I don't think I heard *all* of it, did I, Mrs. Steward?"

"Why," she said, "not—"

"No, Elsie, no!" Steward swung around and faced her. "No! Don't tell! Don't—"

"That's all," Asey said as he broke off. "That's all I wanted to find out, really. I wasn't a bit sure there was any more, but now I know there is."

Steward stared at him speechlessly.

"Furthermore," Asey said gently, "I'm not even goin' to try an' worm it out of you. Because I think you're goin' to tell me, all by yourself. I think you're goin' to be real glad to."

He looked from Steward to Hanson, and then back to Steward. Then he smiled.

"Uh-huh," he said, "I think I can easily foresee the time when you'll practically come to me on your hands an' knees, maybe even pushin' a peanut with your nose for good measure, just to get to me, an' tell me. Now, I'm goin'—can I, Hanson?"

"You're going home to *bed!*" Hanson said. "Oh, yes you are, too! Doctor's orders. You heard what he said. Bed for you!"

"But—"

"Look, you can't hardly stand up on your two feet! I been watching you," Hanson said. "You can't fool me. *I* know! You're trying hard, I'll grant you that, but I can guess how bad you feel. And you don't look so good, either. And you're twitchy. Don't *you* think he's twitchy?" he asked Horner.

"Listen here, the only trouble with me is a little scratch, that's all!" Asey said. "It feels—"

"Oh, come now, Iron Man!" Horner said lightly. "Come, come now! Any more of that 'little scratch' business, and I'll consider you delirious, and treat you accordingly! From where I'm standing, that lump on your cranium doesn't resemble any bitsy little scratch, you know! On the contrary, there's something about your profile that's slightly reminiscent of a two-headed marvel I once saw in a circus side show!"

"I know," Asey said. "It feels like someone'd hung a boxin' glove up there. But—it don't hurt! I haven't even got a headache! It don't bother me at all! It's only that little scratch—"

"Come along!" Horner said briskly. "I'm driving you home! And leave us not argue about it! I don't feel a bit like arguing, and concussion is a dull subject. Come on—oh. I forgot. I haven't got my car!"

"You can take mine," Hanson said. "Sam'll drive you. That's the best way. You can go home with Asey, and then after you're sure he's okay, Sam can drop you off at Cummings's. Then he can bring the car back here, and—"

"Zanies!" Elsie said. "Oh, dear, darling, you shouldn't! That's the doctor's nice bag—I'm terribly sorry, Doctor Horner, it's not that he's vicious or hungry or anything like that, but he loves to chew leather, and particularly *old* leather, like that bag strap. Zanies, darling, stop it!"

"Asey," Horner said, "have you any influence? I am deeply attached to that bag—hey, you, no!" he added as the cat started to climb into the bag. "No, you don't! Get out of that!"

He reached down to remove Zanies.

A second later, his hand was bleeding from his wrist to the tip of his forefinger.

"Oh, dear!" Elsie said. "Oh, dear, I'm terribly sorry, I *do* hope you're not badly hurt—Kemper, get the iodine, quickly! Oh, there's some in your bag, isn't there, Doctor Horner? May I—"

"Don't bother," Horner said with a laugh. "It isn't as bad as it looks, really." He wiped the back of his hand with his pocket handkerchief. "Er—just a scratch, to coin a phrase."

"But a little iodine—"

"It's quite all right, really!"

"Zanies didn't *mean* to!" Elsie said defensively. "I *know* he didn't!"

"Oh, I'm sure he didn't! Probably his mind was on something else entirely. Some other cat, say. Or the meat situation." Horner smiled suddenly, and Asey thought it was about time he sensed that his irony wasn't going over too well with Elsie Steward. "Of course, it was probably my own fault. I probably didn't approach him properly. Or from the right side, or something."

"Well, if you don't *mind* my saying so," Elsie returned, "you really didn't. You pounced, you know. Of course *I* understand how you must have felt about your—what is that word, Kemper? Not exactly *clean?*"

"Sterile?" Steward suggested helpfully.

"That's it. Your sterile bag, and all that. But cats like Zanies are *quite* sensitive, and they simply will *not* be pounced on. It's fatal. They always react—oh, dear, Kemper! Now he's made up his mind to follow you, Mr. Mayo!"

"Zanies, I'll see you tomorrow!" Asey said. "I might even break down an' bring you some of Joe's catnip hoard from the shed if you behave like a good cat—go on, now, leave me be! Behave!"

Zanies looked up at him sulkily, and then began to mew.

"Hush, now! Pipe down that plaintive talk!" Asey said. "Stop sulkin'!" He turned politely to the Stewards. "Good night! You know, Mrs. Steward, I'm sort of sorry that you never happened to meet my cousin Jennie, who keeps house for me."

"I've heard Ann speak of her. She was running that bazaar this afternoon, wasn't she?"

"Uh-huh." Asey paused in the doorway and grinned. "You are the only other person I ever met," he said, "who has Jennie's ability to notice people casually in passin'. Doc Cummings always refers to it as a photographic sense of detail, or camera mind. Jennie is also very fond of cats, too. Good night!"

"Good ni—oh, Zanies, come back here! Kemper, he's following Mr. Mayo again—can't you *do* something? Where's his harness? He simply won't mind me—"

Before Asey was able to leave, Zanies had to be confined in his traveling cage.

His plaintive yowlings were audible even outside on the front steps.

"Gee, what a beast!" Hanson said as he and Horner and Asey started down the gravel walk. "Listen—you can still hear him! Me, I'd as soon think of keeping a tiger in my house! Say, doc, will you hop ahead and yell for Sam?"

"Yell *where?*" Horner demanded shortly.

"Oh, just yell around. Anywhere down there by the garage," Hanson said. "Down around there. Thanks," he added as an afterthought.

"Don't mention it, I'm sure!" Horner retorted. "But you could have achieved the same effect by saying pointedly that you wanted to talk to Asey alone, you know! I'm quite susceptible to little hints!"

Hanson shook his head as the doctor strode off in the direction of the garage.

"These guys just out of the service are a little touchy sometimes, aren't they?" he remarked.

"Wa-el," Asey said, "we're so used to workin' with Doc Cummings, I suppose anyone any younger seems like an errand boy to us, kind of."

"I never meant to *boss* him, Asey!" Hanson said honestly.

"I know. An' I haven't meant to treat him like a little kid, either," Asey said. "But I'm willin' to bet we've both goaded him a little. He seems to know his business all right."

Hanson nodded. "He was talking with Doane, down at the drugstore, about opening his own office in New York after Cummings comes back from his vacation. Said that was why he'd offered to take over here now for the doc, because he was waiting for this new equipment of his to be installed, and all, and he thought practicing down here for a few weeks would be good experience, and like a rest for him, too. Say, Asey. Say—uh—"

"That's all right," Asey said quickly. "I knew you wouldn't cling to that notion forever."

"Honestly," Hanson said, "I can't exactly explain it, but it sounded awfully sensible to me! Not at first. At first it was just another idea, but then—honestly, I can't put it into words! I can't explain it to you. First one person came and told me all about that fight you'd had with Tinsbury, and what you threatened him, and all. And then another person. And then another, and another. And every time somebody *else* told me, why, it got to seeming *more* sensible! I'm not trying to say it was all their fault. It was mine, too. But those other people had something to do with it—gee, I wish I could make you see what I mean! It *did* make sense!"

"I think I got an idea of what you're drivin' at," Asey said. "Cummings lent me a book once—called *Extraordinary Popular Delusions, and the Madness of Crowds,* or something like that. It's what you might sum up as 'Monkey See, Monkey Do,' on a big scale.

Read it some day. It's just about the sort of thing that you ran into, in a small way."

"Why," Hanson said wonderingly, "it sounds crazy to me now —but for a while there, I got to feeling I was dead right, and you *had* murdered Ann Tinsbury!"

Asey chuckled.

"It sounds crazy to me, now, but for a while there I felt some of it, myself," he said. "After I'd been told by a little girl that of course *every*one knew I was guilty—except her papa, who was a mite queer anyway—why, I took to sneakin' through back yards like I'd committed every crime on the books. It's catchin'."

"I'll say! I didn't start to snap out of it until Steward as good as called you a looter and a thief," Hanson said. "That cracked it. I said to myself you weren't anything of the kind, and I knew it. Look, what're we going to do about Steward? I don't want to go off half-cocked any more!"

"I sort of wish," Asey said, "that you'd stay here a while, an' just ask him questions. Ask, an' ask, an' ask, an' ask."

"Okay. What about, though?"

"The same things you already been askin' him. Just keep on with 'em. Ask 'em over an' over. Be polite with him. Don't even raise your voice. But wear him down. Make him feel it'll be a holy relief for him to tell me of his own accord whatever it is he's holdin' back. An' when you go, by the way," Asey added, "be sure an' leave someone behind here to look after that pair. I think they really ought to have a guard."

"They wouldn't dare to run away—oh, I get your angle," Hanson said. "You mean because of this looter, and all those diamonds, huh? What do you think about that fellow, anyway?"

"It seems to be the consensus that there's been some very selective lootin' goin' on," Asey said. "My guess is that this lad's responsible for it. The first edition an' antiques end, I mean. Not just the cook-stoves an' the porch furniture division."

"Some bright boy from the city, huh?" Hanson asked.

Asey shook his head.

"Oh, he must be!" Hanson said. "You didn't recognize him, he apparently didn't recognize you this afternoon, the Stewards didn't know him!"

"I still don't think he's any city slicker," Asey said. "He knows his way around this town pretty good. He knew the inlet woods, an' he knew enough about the marsh to catch me there, by the bridge."

"What bridge?"

"You're provin' my point for me," Asey told him. "You know more or less about the town, as much as most natives, but you don't know enough about the marsh to know about that old bridge! An' he sure knew his way around the Tinsbury house! Knew there was an alarm system, knew just how to silence it. Even knew just where the front door was, an' went straight for it when he made his emergency exit—that's a lot more than I could've done after enterin' from the rear, on my first visit!"

"I see what you mean," Hanson said slowly. "But if he was someone who knew this place so well, then why didn't the Stewards know who he was?"

"I keep feelin' in my bones," Asey said, "that they'd ought to have."

"Think he was wearing a disguise, or something? Oh, after fighting with him, Asey, you'd have known if he was wearing a wig or a false nose!"

"I think it's more a matter of a make-up job," Asey said. "Stain an' grease paint. But I don't think it would do an earthly bit of good to go back an' confuse the Stewards by askin' if they'd have known him if he was blond, say. Hanson, that topaz flower pin in the girl's coat lapel was one of a pair. It could be that this selective looter would be smart enough to take one, an' leave her watch an' money behind."

"Could be, but *I* don't like it," Hanson returned. "It's too damn smart, if you know what I mean."

"Uh-huh, I do. It's almost like someone might have taken one pin, an' hoped that we'd speculate about selective looters. Wa-el," Asey said, "I don't know. Could be she just lost it."

"Say," Hanson stopped by the corner of the garage, "what do you think about Steward? Honestly?"

Asey turned and looked back toward the house.

"Funny thing," he said. "When I looked in at that couple through a fancy plate-glass picture window a while ago, I couldn't imagine 'em guilty of anything more vicious than chiselin' a few dollars off their net income to duck a higher surtax bracket. But when you stand here an' look back at that house, an' think of 'em—"

"And that cat! And look at those trees!" Hanson pointed toward the elms. "They look like hands, don't they? Grabbing— oh, hello, Horner. Got Sam at last? Fine. Thanks a lot. Now, Asey, go on home and go to bed! We can pick this up tomorrow morning!"

"Uh-huh," Asey said.

"I don't trust you," Hanson said. "Doc, you'll get tough with him, won't you?"

"Tough? With *him?*" Horner laughed.

"Yes, *tough!* What you're to do," Hanson said, "is to get him into bed. Give him something to make him sleep, if you have to. Then you can run along home."

Asey knew that he hadn't meant it the way he'd said it, but he could feel Horner stiffen.

"But yes, mon lieutenant!" Horner took off his hat and swept the ground with it as he bowed low. "But yes! Consider it done, but at once, but immediately! And after I've tucked him in, will there not be any other little chores the lieutenant wishes the doctor to perform for him, before he runs along home himself? Haven't you a little washing I could hang out?"

"I only—" Hanson began and then stopped. "I didn't—that is, I just—" he gave up entirely. "No, doc, that's all, thanks. Good night, Asey."

The ride back to Asey's house was very quiet indeed.

Sam, the state cop, was a stranger to Asey, and his conversation consisted entirely of requests for road directions.

Horner, in the back seat, never said a word.

"Hey, blow your horn!" Asey said suddenly.

Sam obediently blew it, and then looked at him curiously.

"Oh-oh, I'm sorry!" Asey said. "I thought that was a car swingin' out of the side lane, but it was only that reflector sign—I forgot about that. An' I didn't mean to backseat drive. Now, you take the next road to the right—"

He greatly doubted if even Horner suspected that the horn had sounded just as they were passing by the spot Jennie had referred to as where the old icehouse had burned down.

When they arrived at Asey's, Horner got out of the car and followed him into the kitchen.

"Look, will you go to bed?" he asked. "I mean, I'm hardly going to stand over you with a razor strap, but I wish you would. Enough so that if you say you won't, I might be inclined to stay here, according to my instructions from the excellent lieutenant."

"I will." Asey felt that he couldn't say much of anything else. After all, he'd tried to make explanations once and got nowhere. The story of that little scratch on his collarbone wasn't going to sound any better now. "I will. I promise you I'll go straight upstairs."

"Good." Horner paused on the threshold. "Sorry I lost my temper," he said lightly. "I'm afraid Hanson has just the slightest tendency to burn me up. It's cumulative, unfortunately. The longer I know him, the more I seem to mind him."

Asey nodded.

"I understand," he said. "He could burn me sometimes, if I'd let him, an' he's often worked your uncle up into a good thick lather. Would it make you feel better, or brighten your life any to know that Cummings an' I have both thrown things at him, over a period of years?"

"I feel much better," Horner said promptly, "and much less like

a fractious child." He laughed. "You know what's really bright-
ened my way and eased my load and kept me amused, during the
grimmer moments of this first day here?"

"What?"

"The fact that I came," Horner said, "for a good rest. Those were
the very words I used to uncle, and I like to think of him screaming with inward laughter. A good rest! Wow!"

"Think nothin' of it," Asey returned. "Look at me. I come home
from the industrial wars, as you might say, kind of expectin' to
revel in peace an' calm an' apple turnovers. Welcome Home, Asey
Mayo, it said on that banner. So far, I been labeled a thief an' a
looter an' a murderer, I been driven to breakin' an' enterin' in the
night, I been biffed over the head, tossed into a mudhole, clawed by
a Siamese cat, an' gone two brisk rough an' tumble rounds with no
holds barred."

"Condensed in that factual fashion, it's a positively awe-
inspiring recital!" Horner said. "It's my obvious duty to give you a
break and carry you bodily upstairs— I will, too, if you'd like. But
at least no one's spent the day comparing you unfavorably with
your uncle, or calling you a cocky little whippersnapper. You've
got that much to be thankful for!"

"Oh, I don't know," Asey said. "There was one point when a
paper hanger I didn't know seemed to be the only friend I had in
the world. Why, there've been times today when I've caught myself thinkin' of the Porter Plant kind of wistful, like—the way I
used to think of home before I got back here. In short, as my cousin
Syl says, you can't never tell what things ain't goin' to happen
almost any minute. Don't let Hanson throw you—good night!"

He stood in the doorway of the kitchen and watched the lights
of the police car disappear down the lane.

Not five minutes later, the jeep came bouncing up into the yard.

"Well!" Jennie said as she bustled in. "Well! I *hoped* it would
be you that blew the horn, because I was pretty near at my wits'
end. And then I realized that it was Hanson's car, so I waited down
at the corner until I saw it leave—what's been happening, for

goodness' sakes? Tell me, quick! Are you arrested, or un-arrested, or what? What's happened?"

"My status has changed," Asey said. "I was just sent home to bed."

"Now look here, Asey, stop fooling! We haven't got much time! Put it," Jennie said, "into a nutshell! What's happened?"

In what amounted to a miracle of brevity, Asey summed things up for her.

"For goodness' sakes!" Jennie said. "But I must say you look all right, except maybe a little lumpy around your head. I'll go get the iodine for those cat scratches right away. It's in my desk. If there's time," she added as she bustled into the dining room, "I'll make you a sandwich. I picked up some food—what time *is* it, anyway? My watch has stopped."

Asey looked at his own watch.

Then he held it to his ear.

Then he shook it.

"Seems to be somethin' wrong with mine, too," he said. "Hey, Jennie, while you're in there, take a look at the electric clock!"

"It hasn't worked since the hurricane," Jennie informed him as she returned with the iodine bottle. "When the electricity went off, something gave a funny click, and I haven't been able to make it start up again. You've got to take it apart—what's the matter with your watch? I never knew that to stop before!"

"It's goin'," Asey said. "It hasn't stopped. It's runnin', all right. Only it's lost four or five hours, I'd say as an offhand guess."

"What does it *say?*" Jennie demanded.

"It's certainly more than two hours ago since I left little Mildred an' her lollypop outside of the movies!" Asey said. "Must be nearly two or three in the morning, now. But this says it's only twenty minutes of ten—an' *that* can't be right!"

"What are you talking about, it must be two or three in the morning? I never heard such nonsense!" Jennie retorted. "Must be that crack on the head and getting knocked out that makes you feel that way. If you'd been rushing around like *I* have, you'd know that it couldn't possibly be more than eight-thirty! Not at the most!"

"Wa-el, let's put on the radio," Asey suggested. "We ought to be able to tell from that."

"Isn't any radio," Jennie said. "The tubes gave out months ago, and I couldn't get any new ones, so I just put it up in the attic. You'll have to—"

"But what about your soap operas?" Asey interrupted. "How in the world've you managed to get along without *Luella's Other Husband,* an' *Sally MacPhee, the Girl Riveter,* an' all those others?"

"I think," Jennie said quite seriously, "that on the whole, I'm a lot happier without 'em. I don't seem to *worry* so much, somehow —I'll go ask the phone girl what time it is. Because it's mighty important that we know for *sure!*"

When she came back, she was struggling to get into her coat.

"Get that left sleeve for me, quick, Asey!" she said as she grabbed the iodine bottle with her right hand. "And put this into your pocket— I'll have to fix up your cat scratches later. Come on, hurry up! Hurry up! Get your hat and come along!"

"What's all this rush about?" Asey asked as she pushed him toward the door. "Where's the fire? What do you think—"

"Oh, come along quick and stop asking fool questions! It's quarter to *ten!*"

"Quarter to *ten?* That's *all?* Then my watch was right all the time?"

"Your watch was right all the time," Jennie opened the door and gave him a shove. "You were hours ahead of yourself, that's all, and it's only just an hour and fifteen minutes later than *I* thought! We've got fifteen minutes—run, can't you? Hurry up! Get into that jeep!"

"But—"

"Sometimes for someone who's supposed to be so awful bright and an old Codfish Sherlock and a Hayseed Sleuth and fiddle-de-dee like that," Jennie said, "you're the stupidest man I ever knew!

Get out of that driver's seat, *I'm* driving! *I* know where we're going! And you hang on, because we're in a hurry!"

"Why?"

"Why? Because he's coming back at ten! I told you we only had fifteen minutes!"

"Who's coming back at ten?" Asey asked as Jennie backed the jeep around and headed it down the lane.

"I don't *know* who!" she snapped. "That's just the whole point, I don't know *who* he was!"

"What's he comin' back at ten *for?*" Asey shouted at her as Junior careened off down the lane. *"Where?"*

"To see Maggie Peeling, stupid!" Jennie turned around and glared at him.

"Oh. Oh—hey, *watch* it, will you?"

"Watch *what?*" Jennie turned her head to the left.

"The road! I'm not nervous, but—"

"Don't be. I'm used to this now. I like it. It's so handy," Jennie slewed onto the main road without pausing. "I *don't* see how I lost that hour and fifteen minutes! Must've been while I was just sitting and waiting by where the old icehouse was. Well, I guess we can make it!"

"Look, Jennie, who's meetin' Maggie Peeling at ten, anyway?"

"I keep telling you, I don't know! He's a dark sort of man, dressed in kind of a tough style, dark sweater," Jennie said, "and dark pants, and no shirt—"

SEVEN

Asey leaned back his head and gave a war whoop, and then he hurriedly reached out and grabbed the wheel and set the jeep back on its course.

"Don't you ever dare scare me like that again!" Jennie said. "I nearly climbed that tree, and I wouldn't have blamed myself if I had! What're you whooping about like a wild Indian? Are you crazy, or something?"

"Covert?" Asey asked. "Covert pants, I mean? Was this fellow wearin' dark covert pants?"

"Why, yes!" Jennie said. "How'd you know? I had to think for the longest time before I remembered the name of the material! Of course, I *had* plenty of time to remember, all hunched up like a jackknife there in that jam closet."

"Funny thing," Asey raised his voice. "Must be Junior bouncin', but it sounded to me just like you said 'jam closet' then."

"I did."

Asey waited until she finished negotiating a reverse curve before he asked her if she didn't think that sounded just a little silly.

" 'Course it does!" Jennie said. "And I certainly *felt* silly! I couldn't think of a sensible answer—I mean, what I'd say if they found me and asked what I was doin' in there. You couldn't just open your mouth and say you'd dropped in for a jar of quince jelly! That was all she had in there, quince."

"P'r'aps it's her favorite. Uh—tell me, Jennie, just when did you spend this little interlude in Maggie Peeling's jam closet, anyway? It was hers, I gather?"

Jennie nodded. "I went right straight over there, after Hanson and Horner left our house. I told you I had my own suspicions about her. There wasn't a soul home, but everything was wide open, so I went right into the pantry and counted the plates. Then, of course, I *knew* I was right in suspectin' her."

Asey drew a long breath. "Counted what plates?" he asked.

"The rosebud plates, of course, what else? I never *did* manage to find out what you did with that one of hers you took away this afternoon and wound that cod line around, but—" Jennie swung the jeep around a corner on half of one wheel. "That's what I *like* about this," she added parenthetically. "You can just turn without havin' to *think* about it first."

"You were discussin' plates," Asey reminded her.

"Oh, yes. Well, whatever you did with that one you had, she's got it back."

Asey opened his mouth to speak, and then closed it again.

"*I* thought," Jennie said, "that you might just posssibly be sort of pleased to know that! Don't you *care* about that rosebud plate any more?"

"I care deeply," Asey said. "Look, can't you pull up for a second an' let me get this straight? If you had fifteen minutes when we left the house, you certainly got eleven an' a half of 'em left right now! Be generous! Let me have your full attention for just a couple of 'em!"

Jennie refused to stop. "I wouldn't *feel* right if I did. I'd fret. But I guess we can afford to slow down a bit. Well, I told you Maggie Peeling had worked her fingers to the bone gettin' a dozen of everything in that hand-painted rosebud set, didn't I? I know just what she's got, every piece, because she's told me all about it. Well, when I went there, I went into the pantry—and there was *twelve* of those plates, the size you had, up there on the shelf! *Twelve* of 'em!"

"So!" Asey said. "So! I s'pose you're sure about that?"

"I counted that pile three times. Not just with my eyes," Jennie said, "I put my finger out and touched 'em. It's simple arithmetic, that's all. If she gave me one, then she had eleven left. But now she's got *twelve*! And I'm certain sure I don't think she went out this afternoon and bought a thirteenth! Her goal was a dozen of the different size plates, she told me. And she didn't have any more than twelve of any other size plate."

"No spares?"

"No spares. So," Jennie said, "she's got back the plate you had." She slowed the jeep down to a crawl and looked at him.

"Uh-huh," Asey said.

"Is that all you can muster up to say? Doesn't this plate business *matter* to you any more?"

"It matters considerable," Asey said. "I was just thinkin', if I was ashamed of myself at the time for sneakin' through back yards, I'm even more ashamed now. Looks to me like you'd been doin' the detectin' in this family! What happened after you counted the plates? How'd you get yourself into a jam closet?"

"Maggie Peeling slipped into that house so quiet," Jennie said, "I didn't hear her until after I'd left the pantry. I kind of ducked into what I knew was the door to the front hall—always *was* the door into the front hall when the Martins owned the house!—but it turned out Mrs. Peeling'd done some remodelin' and rebuildin' and rearrangin' since I was there. Now it was the door into a jam closet—shelves at the top and a cupboardy place at the bottom. There I ducked, and there I was—cornered, and all hunched up like a jackknife, and feelin' such an awful fool!"

"What was she wearin'?" Asey asked. "Blue slacks an' a white jacket like Lois had on? Or didn't you get to see her?"

"Yes, and a red scarf around her hair. She's a writer, you know, and she went over and sat down at her typewriter, and started to bang away at it. I could see a little slice of her through a crack," Jennie explained. "She'd bang a little, and then take out the page and crumple it into a ball, and throw it into the fireplace. Then she'd do it all over again. I must say I don't see, after watchin' her, how she ever gets anything *done!* Far's I could make out, she writes a page and throws it away, and that's all—she doesn't seem to *save* any of it!"

"What's the matter?" Asey asked as she stopped the jeep.

"Nothin', we're here, that's all—or as near as we probably ought to get. That's the house ahead there. I don't see any lights anywhere, though, do you?" Jennie craned her neck.

"Not a glimmer. It isn't ten yet, though," Asey said. "Lacks a couple of minutes. I wish you'd tell me more about this dark fellow, an' what's goin' on here!"

Jennie said she was getting to him as fast as she could, goodness knew, but goodness knew she had to get to it the way it all happened, didn't she? First she had to tell him about Maggie's fight with her sister Lois.

"Over those clothes Maggie had on, that you mentioned. Lois came steamin' in and told her to get out of 'em, quick! And Maggie said, 'Go away, kitten, you bother me!' They had quite a set-to there, Asey. Seems they belonged to Lois, but Maggie'd worn 'em all day, and intended to keep right on wearing 'em. Lois was awful mad—you wouldn't have known her for the same girl in our kitchen. Finally she said Maggie'd probably live to regret not changin' those clothes, and Maggie said 'Run along, little kitten! If you don't like it here, you know what you can do! See if you've any rich friends left who'll take you in. Try it!' "

"You don't make Maggie sound like the pleasantest person I ever heard tell of," Asey remarked. "How old is she?"

"Maybe ten years older than Lois," Jennie told him. "She's dark, and taller, and she's got one of those horrid thin mouths. 'Course it doesn't look thin at first, but if you look under the lipstick, it's a thin, mean, shrewish mouth. She's mixed in with the women here in town, but I've always steered a little clear of her. I think her heartiness, like when she comes to the club, is just a put-on job. It's always been my opinion she was scratchin' up local color for one of her stories."

"What was the difficulty between her," Asey asked, "an' Ann Tinsbury?"

Jennie shook her head. "I never knew. I never asked Ann about it—wasn't any of my business. I do know they hardly nodded to each other when they met. They wasn't what you'd call friends. I know Ann didn't like her—you knew when Ann didn't like people," she added. "Ann wasn't a one to beat about the bush any —here comes a car! And about time!"

But the car sailed past them up the road without stopping.

"After the way *we* flew to get here," Jennie said with an indignant sniff, "it certainly seems to me *they* might be on time! What's keeping 'em? It's certainly after ten o'clock now!"

"Wa-el," Asey said dryly, "you might say they probably aren't takin' us into their considerations any. Look, about Ann an' Lois— I got the impression they got on all right, in spite of Ann an' Maggie, but that Lois kind of had to meet Ann on the sly, like."

"Maggie's doings, I bet!" Jennie said at once. "After hearin' the way she talked to Lois tonight, it's my guess that Maggie's always kept that girl right under her thumb! The way she rubbed it in about Lois livin' here with her—an' I wonder what she meant, Asey, when she told Lois to go join the army again? She sort of flung that after her as Lois was leavin' the room."

"Did, did she? Huh!" Asey said thoughtfully. "That may explain a lot of things that Steward was sayin' about Lois. If Maggie's a woman who rubs things in hard—uh-huh, maybe that's why Lois seems to have what you'd call a tendency to break loose! What happened after she left? What did Maggie do then? Hurry up with your story, for Pete's sakes, before they come!"

"Maggie went on workin' at her typewriter for a few minutes, but she was too mad to think. I could see that. She said a few nasty words under her breath—I had a pretty good idea *what*," Jennie said primly, "but I'm not repeating 'em. Then she went out and slammed the door behind her, so I couldn't hear where she went to. I didn't know where Lois'd gone to, either, but I decided to take a chance. I started to un-hunch myself—and that's how I got to know about those pants being covert."

"Mean the fellow came in then?"

"Came in," Jennie said, "and sat down in the chair square in front of me. I had to crouch there, half hunched and half un-hunched, while he smoked three blessed cigarettes. All I could *see* was covert pant-leg! Then he finally slatted out—thank goodness!

I couldn't have stayed in that closet another five seconds! I don't think I was ever so uncomfortable in my life. I felt like a canned shrimp! All curled up, and packed in at the same time, and—"

"Jennie, get on with what happened," Asey broke in, "before they come back, an' before I go bats!"

"If you wouldn't keep interruptin' all the time, and breakin' in and askin' things," she retorted, "I could have told you all this ten times over! Well, I un-hunched myself out of that closet and went sneakin' out the back way. And out there on the back terrace—it's a little flagstone affair they've added on in the rear—I almost bumped smack *into* Maggie and him. They were talkin' together."

She stopped.

"Well, get on!" Asey said impatiently. "What about? What were they sayin'? This isn't any time for you to pause dramatic, an' wait for effects, you know! This is the part I been yearnin' to know about—what'd they say? What were they talkin' about?"

Jennie shrugged her shoulders.

"*I* don't know!" she said.

Asey didn't trust himself to say anything at all for a moment.

"Uh—how'd you find out about this ten o'clock date business?" he finally asked. "You must have heard a little somethin'!"

"I heard 'em say 'Tinsbury,' " Jennie said. "Even talkin' low as they was, almost in whispers, that name has a hissy sound you can recognize. I heard 'em say 'Steward,' too. Then they doubled up with laughter, and he said he'd be back at ten. Then they laughed some more—I don't like Maggie Peeling, Asey! I don't like anythin' about her, includin' her laugh. It goes with that mean, nasty mouth of hers."

"An' that," Asey said with restraint, "is all you managed to hear?"

"That's all, and *I* certainly thought it was enough!" Jennie said. "*I* just thought to myself I'd get hold of you and have you come back here at ten and see what they were up to. You know who this fellow is?"

"I'm piously hopin'," Asey said, "that he's my looter— I've kind of got to look on him as my special property. He sounds like my looter. I don't see how it could be anyone else. An' if he is, an' if he an' I mix it up again, I want to tell you right now to pick up the nearest large object you see, an' assist me by bangin' him on the head with it as hard as you can bang—don't let yourself get held back by any false humanitarian considerations, either! Just you bang away for all you're worth!"

Jennie promised that she would.

Then she sighed gustily.

"Oh, dear, where *are* they? I know he went off in a car— I didn't see him, but I heard him go. And I know Maggie went back into the house— I saw her, because I was all hunched up behind the glider, and she went right past me. Now by rights, she'd ought to be inside there waitin', and he'd ought to have been back here fifteen minutes ago! If I'd known we was going to have to hang around like this, I could easy have put the iodine on your cat scratches—how are they?"

"Abatin' somewhat. Did you see this Brian that Lois an' the Stewards talked about? Who is he, anyway?" Asey asked curiously. "You never mentioned him."

"Oh. Oh, that young man who stays here!" Jennie's sniff described very eloquently what she felt about the young man who stayed there. "Hm. Him. Well, he's Maggie's star boarder, if you ask me—of course, she's always been very careful to explain that he's only just helpin' her with the details of some story she's writin' about the air force. Or maybe it's about some flier and his girl, or something. This Brian was a flier, but he used to be a newspaper reporter, or a writer of some sort. He's been hangin' around all summer. Funny, nervous fellow. Keeps to himself. He's—"

"He's what?" Asey asked as she hesitated.

"Well, I don't know how to explain what I mean, but Mary Doane's son has the same look on his face. He was a flier, too. You somehow don't feel that they've exactly got caught up with themselves yet."

"Don't happen to know anythin' about him an' Ann, or him an' Lois?"

Jennie gave a little squeal of surprise.

"Goodness me, *I* didn't even know he knew Ann! Or looked at Lois! I've just always thought of him as an unhappy-lookin' fellow that Maggie Peeling was always callin' at to come carry her packages out of the A & P! Asey, I've just thought—hadn't we ought to hide this jeep?"

"Hide Junior? Nope, I don't see why!"

"But aren't you," Jennie asked eagerly, "goin' to let 'em come home, and then sort of sneak *in* on 'em?"

"I done about all the sneakin'," Asey said, "that I intend to do for one night. No reason for me to hide from anyone now—except maybe Horner, who thinks I ought to be in bed. Golly, I *was* goin' to run upstairs, too, now I think of it. I promised him faithful that I would, an' I meant to. 'Course, I was goin' to run right down again—aha, here comes somethin' that looks promisin'. He's slowin' down—"

A beachwagon slewed into the driveway by the side of the little Cape Cod house ahead.

The horn sounded.

At once, a light was turned on indoors.

Then an outside light flashed on at the rear, illuminating the little terrace.

"So!" Asey said interestedly. "Maggie was in there waitin' all the time!"

The driver of the beachwagon got out, walked quickly around to the rear of the vehicle, and started to take down the tailboard.

"Brought somethin' home with him, did he?" Asey went on. "Well, well! Evidence, yet! Let's us stroll over an' look into this, cousin! An' remember," he added, "what I told you about grabbin' some large object if the need arises! I know this fellow!"

He got out of the jeep, cut across the road, and headed toward the driveway entrance, with Jennie pattering excitedly along beside him.

"He's tryin' to drag somethin' out!" Jennie whispered. "Look— is it *fur*niture?"

It turned out to be a small chest.

Jennie gave a little exclamation of disappointment.

"Oh, only a *box!* Looks like our old croquet set box! *I* thought it might be somethin' excitin'!" She came to a halt as Asey stopped. "Must be awful *heavy,* though, the time he seems to be havin' with—"

"Ssh! Not so loud!"

"Anyway," Jennie obediently lowered her voice till Asey could hardly hear her, "there he *is!* Dark sweater, dark pants. Well, I s'pose we should ought to be glad that it's *him!*"

"Uh-huh," Asey said. "I s'pose."

Because it looked like him, he thought to himself. It certainly looked like him.

But he knew, even at this distance, that it wasn't at all.

It couldn't be.

The fellow he now thought of as his looter would have had that box out with one hand a full minute ago.

With half a hand.

Two fingers.

And this fellow here was still struggling to drag it from the beachwagon's floor onto the tail.

When he did finally manage to get a grip on it, and lift it out, he let it fall again almost at once.

"My God!" Maggie Peeling spoke irritably from the doorway, "can't you even manage *that?* Here, I'll come and get it—look out of the way!"

"Sorry." The man sounded breathless. "It's the width. It really isn't *heavy* at all. I can get it now, I think—"

"Oh, look out, helpless! I'll do it!"

Maggie and the man both leaned over and lifted the box at the same time.

Then, as each looked up and realized that the other had it, the inevitable happened.

They both let go.

The box landed on Maggie's foot, and for a moment the air took on a violent purple hue.

Jennie's tongue began to cluck reproachfully.

"Tch, tch tch! Such language! Almost might think she'd shipped before the mast, wouldn't you, or maybe worked in a stable! Did 'you *ever*—"

But Asey had left her side and was striding forward toward the couple.

Reaching down, he picked up the box with one hand, and with the other he gave Maggie a little shove toward the back door.

"Get along inside with you, Mrs. Peeling!" he said. "I'm in a hurry! You, too, Brian—what's your last name, anyway?"

"Lemoyne." He paused and then added, almost involuntarily, "Sir."

"Get in, Lemoyne. Now hurry up, both of you. Come on, Jennie!"

"Who are you?" Maggie demanded angrily. "Put that box down! That box doesn't belong to you!"

"He's Asey Mayo, that's who!" Jennie said. "And it doesn't belong to you either, I bet!"

"Get in!"

Even though they didn't respond with any particular pleasure, Maggie and Brian at least responded to Asey's quarter-deck voice. They went in.

Still carrying the box under his arm, Asey herded them into the living room.

"Sit down, you two." He put the box down on a cobbler's bench in front of the fireplace, and shook his head as he looked around the room. "Some day," he said, "someone may explain to me why you outlanders insist on paintin' the walls of Cape Cod houses this squeamish color *pink*. Sit down, Jennie, just push a few spinnin' wheels an' butter firkins out of the way— I'm only glad old Cap'n Abner East is in his grave. If the poor old soul ever saw what'd happened to his best parlor!"

"I forgot it was East's!" Jennie said. "Did you notice the ceilin', Asey? *Blue!*"

"I'm tryin' hard not to let it bother me. Neither," Asey said, "am I lookin' at the picture over the fireplace. I like my haddock fresher'n that. Now—"

"What's the meaning of this?" Maggie demanded. "What do you think you're *doing?*"

"Don't bluster, Mrs. Peeling!" Asey said. "From here on, you're a passenger—what's wrong, Jennie, what's the matter?"

"His hair!" she pointed to Brian Lemoyne. "That's why I never recognized him! His hair's really light, but he's done something to it to make it darker!"

"Uh-huh, an' he's used cork liberal on his eyebrows, too," Asey said. "He's had a lot of fun with himself. I know." He reached down and opened the wooden box in front of him. "Well, well!"

The box was stuffed full of letters.

And the letters were, to judge from those on top, all addressed to King Tinsbury.

Just to make reasonably sure, Asey pulled a couple from the bottom and looked at them.

"All right!" he said. "Start talkin', Lemoyne! What's the idea here? Where'd you get these letters of King Tinsbury's?"

"From—" Brian hesitated. "From the Tinsbury house."

"When, tonight?"

Brian nodded.

"How long ago?" Asey snapped out the question as if he were cracking a whip.

"Oh—oh, an hour or so."

"An' who let you in?"

"Ann. Ann Tinsbury," Brian said promptly.

"But she—" Jennie began.

"Hush!" Asey said. "So Ann Tinsbury let you in, an hour or so ago, an' gave you these letters of her father's? I see! An' just what's the reason for this masquerade, anyway?"

"Oh, my God!" Maggie said impatiently, "it was just a joke! We got so sick and tired of hearing about looters and looting, we thought we'd have some fun, that's all! So Brian dressed up the way we heard the looter looked! It's just a joke, that's all! I can't see why there should be all this silly nonsense! After all, Brian didn't *steal* the letters, Ann *gave* them to him—" she broke off as Lois appeared in the doorway. "Oh, hello, kitten! What're you standing out there for? Come in!"

"I'm all right here, thanks."

Lois had changed her clothes, Asey noted. She looked incredibly young in the coral-colored dress she was wearing now. And she'd been crying.

"Come *in!*" Maggie said. "Come in here, little sister! This is apparently some more of your friend Ann Tinsbury's work—I gather she's sent the local Sherlock Holmes here to third degree us! I suppose it's her idea of hilarious humor, to give Brian the letters, and then do a thing like this! Come in!" She raised her voice. "I said, come *in!* Why don't you?"

"I heard," Lois said. "But I'm staying right here. I want to watch this from the outside, as if it were a play. I've been waiting for it for a good many years."

"For what? What are you talking about?"

"For what's coming to you, Maggie." Lois settled herself against the white woodwork. "Go on, Asey, I didn't mean to interrupt."

"Why'd you rush off?" Asey asked. "To warn her about those clothes?"

Lois nodded. "Yes, but she wouldn't listen. I'm sorry I made the effort, now. On the other hand, I've come to, suddenly, about a lot of things. Maggie, I'll give you the only break you're going to get. I'll tell you not to play with him. You're licked!"

"I don't know what you're talking about, sister! And I think for your own good that you'd better come in here and sit down! I—"

"Okay, Mrs. Peeling," Asey said. "That'll do. Sit an' gaze up at that portrait of a haddock. Contemplate it silently. That's your story, Lemoyne? Ann gave you those letters? Goin' to stick to that?"

"Yes!"

Asey looked at him for a moment, and then he turned to Lois. "What d'you think about all this?" he asked. "Think he has any idea what he's doin'?"

"Did you ever carry a torch for anyone?" Lois returned.

"She means, Asey," Jennie said hurriedly, and in a slightly perturbed voice, "were you—"

"I know what she means!" Asey said with a laugh. "Sure, I s'pose so. Most folks have, at one time or another in their lives."

"Not," Lois went on, "that I mean to pry into your personal life, Asey. I just wondered if you knew how you feel when you've just tossed the torch into the ash can. It's a beautiful feeling of freedom. You have a brand new perspective. If you'd asked me that question about Brian this afternoon, I'd have said no, of course Brian didn't know what he was doing! I'd have said that Maggie sent him to Tinsbury's on a fool's errand, and that he went. I'd have built up defenses for him, and alibis. I'd have insisted that he could have gone there and filched these letters for her, and—"

"Lois!" Maggie jumped to her feet. "You—"

Asey pointed to the chair.

"Sit down!"

The quarter-deck voice worked again. Maggie sat down.

"I know where the letters were," Lois continued. "In King's old study on the first floor. All Brian had to do was to open a window —without setting off the alarm! And I'd have claimed that he could do just that without knowing about—"

"About anythin'?" Asey interrupted swiftly.

"Yes. I'd have screamed from the rooftop that it was just the luck that follows the innocent," Lois said, "that he never found out while he was there. I'd have torn my hair out about all this, and patches of my scalp besides, and I'd have believed every word of it, too."

"In short," Asey said, "you'd have said that Maggie pulled the wool over his eyes?"

"She knit a nice thick afghan over 'em. That," Lois said, "is what I *would* have said. But without the glow from that torch, I am not so sure, Asey. My mind's stopped defending him. He's not a valiant hero invalided home from the wars, any more. Or the gay, slapdash, sparkling reporter. He's the man who went overboard for Ann Tinsbury, and used to come and tell me about it by the hour—just what he said to her, and how she slapped him down."

"How he looked into her eyes," Asey suggested, "an' how she blacked 'em?"

"Exactly! Of course he never bothered," Lois said with an honest grin, "to look into mine! Yes, he's the weakling who let Maggie talk him into coming down here. He fell like a ton of bricks for the wonderful opportunities to revive his health and sagging spirits. Of course he never bothered to look beyond her magnificent humanitarianism and realize that she only wanted to use him as a wedge to get to King Tinsbury! She knew that King had always liked Brian, you see, and she's had that book on her mind for years and years!"

"What book?" Asey asked.

"Oh, didn't you know about that? Maggie wanted to write a book about King. *From Rags to Riches,* or *The Last of the Tycoons,* or something. One of those smart biography jobs with a slant —you make it highly significant that someone doesn't like oatmeal, and then you show how it molded 'em. You know. That sort of thing."

"What was King's reaction?" Asey wanted to know.

"What would you expect? He wouldn't have any part of it when she first suggested it," Lois said, "or since. After he died, she tried to work on Ann—she wanted personal stuff, you see. But Ann got simply furious with her about it. They had a terrific battle. Practically a hair-pulling before they got through."

"So *that* was it!" Jennie said. "So that's why they acted so—oh, I'm sorry, Asey, I didn't mean to interrupt and butt in!"

"In fact, Maggie girl," Lois went on before Asey had a chance to speak, "you just about stopped short of blackmailing her, didn't you? And then you made the error of threatening her!"

This time, Asey shoved Maggie back into her Hitchcock chair without bothering first to tell her to sit down and keep quiet.

"She was annoyed enough with you," Lois said, "to write her lawyers a honey of a letter. She told them that no lies you might manufacture could scare her, and that if you wrote just one little paragraph about King and it appeared in print, they were to raise hell—with the publication if they possibly could, and with you anyway. You were going to get it in the neck!"

"You never told me that!" Maggie said angrily.

"No, sister mine," Lois said. "I just sat here hoping you'd take the fatal step. Well, Asey, to get back to the point—Maggie wanted Brian to help her on the Tinsbury book business. He was her wedge."

"Why didn't she use you," Asey asked, "since you got on with Ann so well? Oh, I forgot. Ann wasn't here till recently, was she?"

"No, and I had no influence with King, or with the Stewards. Or with Ann herself, for that matter, although we got on well enough. And Maggie was jealous enough of our friendship to make things hard for me—I had to lie about seeing her, and pretend I hadn't, and all. You guessed that, didn't you?"

Asey nodded.

"Maggie didn't like my being where she couldn't get herself. Brian was her real wedge," Lois said. "I'm not at all sure Maggie didn't want him for herself, too. He ran errands so nicely, and carried home the groceries, and brought in the kindling!"

She stopped and looked at him critically, and then she shook her head slowly.

"How silly you look with that stuff on your face! I hope you feel silly, Brian. You should. You've let her boss your soul out of you when you ought to have gone back to the city, and worked. You're perfectly well. Dr. Cummings said so. You've just got into the habit of babying yourself—the night of the hurricane, you never thought about your stiff arm, did you?"

"I—well—"

"No, you didn't! You worked like a dray horse that night, and you were fine the next day!" Lois said. "But Maggie's encouraged you to sit here and 'think things out.' "

Her imitation of Maggie's voice, Asey thought, was nothing short of brutal.

"She's only let you think of the past," she went on. "Never of the future. And you've swallowed it all whole! You've wallowed in self-pity—about Ann, and about the war, about your arm, about the book you were going to write before the army came into your life! Oh, you've had such a lovely time with your little soul sufferings!"

"I have not! I haven't stayed here willingly!" Brian said. "I haven't liked it!"

"No? I don't recall your kicking and screaming to get away, and out from under Maggie's thumb!"

"What about yourself?" Brian retorted. "I never heard you say a word to her until now!"

"It's this new perspective!" Lois said. "It's doing wonders for me. I don't care any longer what she tells you about me—things you don't know, like my being kicked out of the army. And it mattered to me before, you see, very much. That was one of the reasons why I've knuckled down."

"Sort of had the Indian sign on you, huh?" Asey inquired.

"Oh, she's held so much over me, so long! She's the original I'll-tell-mother-if-you-don't girl! But I've left all that behind. It doesn't matter any more. I heard their plans about this letter business," she added. "Maggie was making it out such jolly fun, to try and get these old letters of King's, while dressed up as the looter. I don't know, of course, how much of it was for effect, in case I happened to be listening, but they certainly were roaring over how peachy it all was!"

"I saw 'em doublin' up with laughter," Jennie said. "Maggie was snickerin' all the way back into the house—oh, sure," she said airily as Maggie stared at her blankly, "sure, I was here!"

"Wa-el," Asey said, "there's still the question I asked you, Lois. Does Brian know what he's doin' for himself by tellin' that yarn?"

"I told you what I'd have said if you'd asked me that this afternoon, and now I'll tell you for now," Lois said. "I don't see how he could have been taken in by any gag about those letters of King's. He knew Maggie'd give her soul for 'em. I don't see how he could help knowing about Ann! I don't see how he has the audacity to pretend, considering the torch he carried for *her* so long, that he doesn't know or doesn't care that she's been murdered. I think it's all brazen, stark lying!"

"Murdered?" Brian got to his feet. "Murdered—Maggie, d'you hear that? Murdered! Ann—murdered? Ann's been murdered!"

"I'm tired," Asey said, "of pushin' people down into their seats. Just sit all by yourself, will you?"

"But—but Ann! Look, I never knew!" Brian said. "When? When did it happen? I was at the beach all afternoon, helping an old lady rescue a hen coop—"

"I'm sure you were very goodhearted an' charitable, too," Asey said. "Probably you fed some poor dog a bone. But you had your say. You're through. You went to Tinsbury's, an' Ann herself give you these letters in the box. That's your story, an' you're stuck with it—or do you maybe want to change it?"

"He's not the police, Brian!" Maggie said quickly. "He's nothing—he doesn't matter! Don't let him rattle you into saying anything! He doesn't count!"

"I have a bucket of badges at home that says I do count," Asey said, "an' I have my cousin an' your sister as witnesses. What about it, Lemoyne, do you want to change your story?"

Brian looked from Lois to Maggie, and then back to Asey.

He didn't say anything. He didn't seem quite able to say anything.

"Okay," Asey said briskly. "That's that! Now, let's see what your story is, Mrs. Peeling. I bet it'll be good, too. I always have a lot of respect for the way you writers—now, what's that term? Think out loud, that's it! You all think out loud so fine! First, though, tell me what you were doin' down in the inlet woods this afternoon, walkin' back an' forth an' back an' forth. Lost somethin', maybe?

Or do you think out loud better when you walk that way, in lines?"

"I never was there!" Maggie said.

"Oh, yes, you were!" Lois said. "He saw you, and I know you were there, and he knows I know you were there! Don't be a sucker, Maggie!"

"I tell you, I wasn't there!"

"Okay," Asey said. "You weren't there. Now, what about the rosebud plate?"

"What," Maggie returned, "about *what* rosebud plate? I have a lot of them, you know. Dozens and dozens. Go look in the pantry."

"He means that rosebud plate," Jennie said, "that you gave me with your turnovers on it, for the cake sale and lawn fête!"

"I think you must be mistaken!" Maggie managed a very creditable smile. "I'd never let one of those plates out of my house, not after the trouble I had laboriously collecting them one by one! I gave you turnovers on a plate that had roses on it, and I remember asking you to be very careful of it—but it wasn't one of my best rosebud set! Not that set!"

"Watch it, puss, watch it!" Lois said. "You're practically digging your grave with your teeth!"

"Go look at the set!" Maggie said. "Count it! You'll find it's all there!"

Asey smiled.

"An' what," he said, "did you do with the cod line, I wonder? Take it back to the store?"

"Cod line? What cod line?" Maggie asked.

"The cod line," Lois said, "that you were marking out the boundary of your new land with! *That* cod line! You know, sister, which line!"

"*Are* you crazy?"

"No, she's not!" Brian said suddenly. "*I* know what cod line Lois means—I carried it out of the hardware store for you last week! You got miles of it. And for just the reason Lois says—to mark the bounds of that new lot you bought over by the inlet woods! I waited an hour out in front of Snow's while they measured that line! I—did you say something?" he asked Asey.

"I was just murmurin' to myself in a philosophic fashion," Asey told him. "I *thought* about bound-markin'. An' passed it up for bein' too simple—an' the end wasn't weighted down! Well, Mrs. Peeling, that much's straightened out! Where's the line now? What did you do with it? Come, come! Where is it?"

"I'm sure I don't know what you're fussing so—"

"I know!" Brian said. "Or at least, I can guess! *That's* what you were burying out back this evening! I asked what you were doing with the trowel, and you said something about transplanting holly-hocks!"

"And so I was! You'll find, if you want to dash out into the night and look, that that's just exactly what I *was* doing, transplanting hollyhocks!"

Maggie sat back and lighted a cigarette.

There was just a hint of triumph in the way she blew out her match, Asey thought. Mentally, he handed it to her. She'd thought of just about everything.

Except, he hoped, one little detail.

"I s'pose," he said, "if you didn't use the cod line for markin' bounds, you didn't use it for anythin' else, did you? I mean, it's just the way you bought it, isn't it? Just the way you brought it home from the store?"

"That's probably the only really sensible question any of you has asked for a long time," Maggie answered coolly. "Yes, of course! It's just the way I bought it, wrapped up in brown paper—it's out in the garage, on the tool bench. Run get it, sister dear!"

Five minutes later, Lois handed the brown paper package to Asey.

"Open it!" Maggie said. "Go on, open it! Do let's get this silly nonsense straightened out! I *still* don't pretend to know what the line has to do—"

She stopped, and watched Asey's face.

"I know," he said. "I hadn't ought to be grinnin', had I? I ought to be pretty mournful an' long-faced. You done fine, Mrs. Peeling.

I already give you a little prize for quick thinkin'. There's only one trouble, you know. Just one little thing!"

"What d'you mean?" Maggie demanded. "You haven't opened it! Go on—open it! You'll find the line in there, just the way I bought it!"

"Uh-huh. I bet." Asey said. "I bet. All coiled nice an' professional, too. But you slipped up!"

"If you won't open it, I'm sure I don't know how you can stand there leering so smugly! You'll find that cod line—every last inch of it—inside that package! Just the way,". Maggie said, "I bought it! Just the way it came from the store!"

"Uh-huh," Asey said gently. "Only—from the *wrong* store!"

"What?"

The question came like a chorus.

"Brian said he waited outside of Snow's," Asey explained. "But the gummed tape on the ends of this package says ELDREDGE'S GEN-ERAL STORE. POCHET FOUR CORNERS. That's the sort of thing I was tryin' to tell you about earlier, Lois," he added. "You go an' get yourself involved this way, an' there's always some one little thing you slipped up on, an' always someone to find it! An' then that one little thing gets proved a phony, an' whoosh—the rest of your story falls just like a card house! If only Maggie'd told the clerk to use string! But she was too busy thinkin' about what was inside the package, I s'pose, to think as hard about the outside of it. She—"

"Duck!" Jennie said.

Asey ducked.

The old Canton ginger jar sailed past his head and thudded into one of the shelves of the walnut whatnot standing in the corner.

For the next few seconds, the room was full of the sound of fall-ing knickknacks.

"An' to think it never even made a dent in that awful pink wall!" Asey said sadly. "Don't try any of that stuff again, Mrs. Peeling, will you? It don't pay. You've only gone an' smashed to smither-eens a lot of imitation Sandwich glass hens—"

"They weren't imitation! They were real! I know!" Maggie said.

She seemed more stung by that casual comment of his, Asey thought, than by anything else he'd said.

"You see how she works," Lois said. "Murder doesn't evoke any particular response in her, but you've stabbed her to the core by insinuating that her Sandwich hens are fakes, and that she got taken in!"

"That glass is real! It's—"

"I'm sorry," Asey said, "it's fake—the kind they used to give away inside those large round packages of oatmeal years ago. Some day, if an' when you're at large, I'll be happy to show you what real Sandwich hens look like. Anyway, no more theatricals, please!"

"Those hens—"

"Those hens've had their day. Let's us get on," Asey said. "When did you go over to Pochet, Mrs. Peeling? This afternoon, I s'pose, after you'd reeled up that first line you'd bought, an' started in to do some heavy thinkin' about truth an' consequences?"

When Maggie gave no indication of hearing his question, let alone answering it, Asey turned and pointed to Brian.

"Do you know?"

"Yes. We drove over there this afternoon, late," he said. "She told me she had things to get there that she couldn't get here in town, and besides, she wanted to have supper at that clam chowder restaurant on Main Street. I think I see now why for once in my life with Maggie I was *not* given a package to carry! I even automatically put my hand out for it, too. I remember that."

"And now *I* see," Lois said, "why I couldn't get hold of either of you on the phone. Well, sister, it was smart work, going to the next town for a new batch of line, so there wouldn't be any curious talk of why you wanted to buy more line here, after you'd just invested in so much mileage! I frankly confess to feeling a repulsive sort of admiration for the way your mind worked things out!"

"You took that sentiment," Asey said, "right off the tip of my tongue! So, Mrs. Peeling, you met Ann Tinsbury, along there on that path in the inlet woods—an' what happened? More arguments an' more hair pullin' about the book you wanted to write about King?"

Again, Maggie didn't seem to hear him.

"Come, come!" Asey said. "I told you I was in sort of a hurry! Speak up, please!"

"Maybe," Brian said, "she'll break down and tell *me* something I'm yearning to know! *Did* you know, Maggie, when you sent me off to steal those letters—did you know then that Ann had been murdered? Did you? There's nothing I can *do* about it now. I'd just like to know. For the record."

Maggie looked up at him and smiled.

"No, Brian, I didn't know!" she said. "But why didn't *you* tell *me* about her, before you went?"

"Oh, stop it, Maggie!" Lois said. "Stop it! I've warned you and warned you!"

"Yes, and I've had about enough," Maggie returned, "of this idiocy from you! *You* left here this afternoon to meet Ann, little sister! I heard you phone and tell her you'd meet her on the way to the post office! And, to borrow Mayo's useful phrase, what happened then? Did you talk about Brian, perhaps? Did you finally realize that Brian would never look at you as long as Ann was alive? Did your great unrequited love finally emerge in all its bitter fury, and strike her down?"

"That's all!" Lois's voice was like the sharp edge of a knife, Asey thought. "That's about all, Maggie girl! Any more, and little sister will have one of her horrider tantrums!"

Maggie leaned back in the Hitchcock chair.

"And very fine tantrums they are, too!" she said. "Mayo would doubtless enjoy watching one." She turned to Asey. "What's the matter, my fine Codfish Sherlock, doesn't Lois count? Why not ask her about these things? She can't deny that she met Ann this afternoon!"

"Did you?" Asey asked.

Lois nodded slowly.

"An' what did you talk about?"

"Brian."

"All right, all right!" Brian said explosively. "Now, ask me! Yes, I met Ann, too! After you did, Lois! And before you ask what we talked about, I'll tell you! We talked about Lois!"

Asey surveyed the trio thoughtfully, and then he grinned at Jennie.

"D'you s'pose you could manage to keep this bunch from cuttin' each other's throats for a few minutes?" he asked. "I want to call Hanson—where's your phone, Lois, in the hall?"

Hanson, he discovered, had already left the Tinsbury house.

And Sam, who'd been left behind as a guard, didn't know where he'd gone.

"Could be to the doctor's, maybe," he added. "That cat scratched him. But I think he was going to find a room in town to spend the night here in. He said he was too damn tired to drive back up the Cape—he's been out since early morning, you know, and all this hurricane stuff's worn him down. He hasn't had any rest since it. He told me I was to call back to Jameson if I wanted anything, or if anything came up."

Asey slowly replaced the receiver.

He didn't want to call Horner. While it was all right for Hanson to know that he was still fooling around with this Tinsbury business, young Dr. Horner had had quite a day of it, he thought. It might just conceivably irritate the fellow a lot to discover that his seriously given professional advice had been so blithely ignored.

"I don't think," he murmured to himself, "that I want to be the last straw. He'd probably rather be called a whippersnapper than be ignored! Huh! Now, I wonder if I—"

He stood out in the hall for a moment and looked into the pink-walled living room.

Maggie Peeling was standing by the fireplace, smoking a cigarette in a long holder, and apparently learning by heart the zigzags in the decorative border of a hooked rug across whose center someone had lovingly hooked the words A PRESENT FROM SARAH P. TUBMAN.

Hunting around in his mind for an adjective with which to sum her up, Asey decided that "seething" would do as well as any.

Lois, now sitting stiffly on a battered horsehair sofa, was seething too, but whether at Brian or at Maggie, Asey couldn't tell. Probably both, he decided. Probably the reaction was setting in now, and she wanted to kick herself for letting Brian know what she had felt about him. She was studying a hooked rug named OUR HOME.

And Brian was seething, too. But somehow, Asey thought, as he watched the fellow walk across to a tobacco jar on the mantel, he was standing straighter, and he didn't look sulky any more.

It occurred to him, as Brian returned to his chair, that he was tall. Taller than he himself had begun to realize at first. Tall enough to approximate Jameson's specifications about Ann's murderer.

Asey shook his head.

They'd all, every last one of them, apparently seen Ann that afternoon.

Who had seen her last?

Hanson, he decided, could tackle that one!

Hanson would do better with the lot of them. He'd bully Maggie, he'd get Brian sore, and he'd infuriate Lois.

The thing for him to do now, he concluded, was to track Hanson down. If Sam were right about his getting a room in town, finding him wouldn't be any more involved than checking up on driveways to see in which particular one his car was parked.

He'd find Hanson, tell him the story, and let Hanson go to work on them. Let Hanson get these three sore enough, and the truth might well come out. Particularly after this general state of seethe abated, and they began to get afraid.

He caught the look Brian shot at Maggie, and the look Maggie darted at Lois, and the look that Lois returned, with interest.

Any one of them, he thought, would have cut through the armor plate of a Porter tank!

"Jennie!" he beckoned for her to come out into the hall. "Come here—in the dinin' room. Listen, I sort of hate to ask you, but d'you think you could keep it up, this state of passive belligerency? I want to go find Hanson an' bring him back here to work on 'em. Think you'd be equal to it?"

"I can try!" Jennie said. "Uh—what'll I *do?*"

"You can't honestly do very much if any one of 'em decides to beat it," Asey said. "Just let 'em bolt. They won't get far. An' I don't think in their present mood that they'd do any pairin' up! Just don't let 'em get *at* each other, that's all! Keep 'em from violence!"

"That's all right to *say,* keep 'em from violence!" Jennie retorted. "Only *how?*"

"Think back to your days in the Ladies' Defense League," Asey suggested. "You used to know how to repel boarders—I mean, invaders—at the drop of a hat, didn't you?"

"You mean all those things I learned to do with handbags and umbrellas?" Jennie said dubiously. "And diggin' your heels into people's shins, and breakin' their arm with that little snap?"

"Any of 'em. Anything but eye gougin', I'd say—oh, don't look so worried! Just keep bearin' in mind that no two of 'em could ever get together long enough to gang up on you, an' that you're more'n the equal of any one. Here, I'll fix things for you!"

He reached out, removed a candle from its pewter holder, and held it out to her.

"Here—put this in your pocket. Now you got a gun," he said. "Come along, now!"

"What are we playing now?" Maggie demanded acidly as they returned to the living room. "Word games? Do we guess what word—"

"Get over to that!" Asey pointed to the old-fashioned melodeon standing against the wall. "Sit down! Now, play it!"

"Play what?"

"I don't care. Hymns," he said, "might maybe be sort of helpful at this time. Just play, an' keep on playin'. Lois, you an' Brian will sit just where you are, an' listen. I'll break it to you that I've given Jennie my gun. Jennie once tried to learn how to use a gun when she was in the Ladies' Defense League, but she wasn't awful good.

She has a very nervous trigger finger. I think you will all be very wise to mind her till I get back!"

The slightly frenzied wailing of the melodeon followed him as he left the house.

He stopped long enough by the beachwagon in the driveway to take out the keys, and then he reminded himself that a similar gesture hadn't apparently inconvenienced Hanson a whit.

Maybe Maggie also had spare keys handy!

"Huh!" he said. "Whyn't I take this, myself? Just as easy—"

But after starting it, and prudently noting that the gasoline gauge registered only a hair's breadth above 'Empty,' he merely drove the beachwagon up the road to where the jeep was parked, and then removed the keys.

"There!" he said as he got into Junior. "If they want to drive two an' a half miles away from here badly enough, that'll at least make it harder for 'em to start! Now, Junior, let's get on with locatin' Hanson!"

About a mile up the road, his headlights picked up a plump little figure in dungarees and a tentlike white sweater trudging on ahead.

"For Pete's sakes!"

Asey slowed down and stopped beside Mildred.

"Hi," he said. "For Pete's sakes, what're you doin' out wanderin' around in the middle of the night like this for?"

Mildred giggled as though he'd said something terribly funny.

"Why, it *isn't* the middle of the *night!*" she said. "It isn't a bit late, Mr. Mayo! Only a little after eleven—the show's just out! It was a double feature!"

Asey looked at his watch.

"Huh!" he said in some surprise. "Seems like I'm wrong again, an' you're right! But eleven-twenty's still too late for you to be strollin' around by yourself! Hop in. I'll take you home. Whereabouts do you live?"

Mildred gave a joyous little squeal, but then she drew back.

"It's all right, I'm not a suspected murderer any more," Asey assured her. "Your papa was right. I'm not only socially acceptable,

I'm practially the forces of law an' order, now. Hop in—where do you live?"

"Well," Mildred still hesitated. "Well, I suppose it's all right, and I've *wanted* to ride in that jeep ever since I saw it in your yard, Mr. Mayo. It's only those things mother said about not ever taking rides at night from—but I know papa wouldn't mind!" She suddenly hopped up beside him. "I live on Mill Road!" she added a little breathlessly.

"*Mill* Road? But child, aren't you kind of out of your way, over here?" Asey asked curiously. "Must be a good mile an' a half longer to Mill Road, comin' around this way, than if you'd taken the other fork, just below the movie theater!"

Mildred giggled some more.

"*I* know!" she said delightedly. "*I* know!"

"What's the idea?" Asey asked as he started up Junior.

"Well," Mildred was so shaken with giggles, she almost couldn't bring herself to speak, "well—well, if you really want to *know*—it's my *boy* friend!"

"Oh. Oh, I see. An' he lives around this way, does he, huh?"

"No!" Mildred jumped up and down. "Oh, *no! He* lives over in the *Center!*"

"I always guessed I was an awful punk detective," Asey said. "I don't get it!"

"Why, he leaves me *letters,* of course! I was going home this way to see if he'd left one!"

"Oh." Asey said. "Oh! Of course! Where's he leave 'em?"

"In the old mailbox that's standing all by itself below the Anderson farm," Mildred told him. "*Nobody* ever uses it but *us!* It's so old, you can't even tell what name was on the side once. And it squeeeeeeks, like that!" she demonstrated the sound. "When you open the door, I mean. It's *won*derful! It makes me shiver. Er—*you* could hear it, if you liked."

"So?"

"Yes, it's *only* right up ahead a little ways. I don't suppose you'd want to stop, though."

"I s'pose I might's *well*," Asey said. "It'd be pretty awful if your letter was there all night, wouldn't it? Sing out before we come to it —only don't get so excited you fall out first!"

"I won't, but I got to watch—there! Over there, see?"

Asey pulled the jeep across the road, and drew up alongside the box.

"There," he said. "We don't even have to get out. Shall I open it, or do you want to?"

"*You* can," Mildred said generously.

"Thanks."

It squeaked very nearly as stridently as she had claimed, and she shivered luxuriantly.

"Gee, I'm sorry," Asey said as he felt inside. "The boy friend seems to've let you down, Mildred. It's empty!"

"Did you look *all* the way in?" Mildred clambered past him and groped around inside the box with a fat little hand. "Sometimes he puts it *way* back to be funny—oooh!"

"Hey, you'll fall!"

"Oooh, candy! Candy! Look, a square box!"

"Let me get that," Asey said, "before you break your little neck!"

"Is it mints?" Mildred asked as he drew out a square glass box. "Mints? Is it—"

But Asey was standing in front of the headlights, examining a square glass container in which there reposed a square plum pudding, embellished with a sprig of holly on top!

EIGHT

"OH, that ole thing!" Mildred sounded as though she were going to cry. "Ooh! And I thought it was *candy* from *Freddie!* And now someone *knows* about our mailbox! Now it doesn't *count* any more! That ole darn pudding!"

The reactions of torch-bearing women, Asey thought, were more or less universally similar. He let her cry it out.

When her sobs subsided to sniffles, he silently offered a handkerchief, which she silently accepted.

"I don't s'pose," he said tentatively, "that you'd know anythin' about this darn ole puddin', would you? I don't s'pose you'd happen to know who brought it to my house today, would you, or who left it there?"

"No," Mildred said, "I don't know who *brought* it or *left* it, but I know who *made* it, and I know who put it in our *box!* Always spoiling things, the old *Prune*face! She never liked Freddie—that's my boy friend's name—because he put that frog in her desk when she was teaching his class that time Miss Benton was sick! Well, I'll get *back* at her for finding out about our letter box, I bet you! I'll *show* her, I bet you!"

She gave her plump little face a final, decisive wipe, and handed the handkerchief back to Asey.

"Thanks. And it squeaked so wonderful!" she said with a sigh. "Don't you think she's *mean,* spoiling everything? The old *Prune*-face! Honest, don't you think she's *horrid?*"

Asey told himself to proceed with patience and caution. While he could hardly explain to little Mildred what he knew about the pudding, it looked as though she might be able to tell him a lot.

" 'Course," he said, "bein' away like I have, I don't know which Pruneface you mean. There's so many Prunefaces around."

"Oh, *I* mean Miss *Curran!*"

The square plum pudding very nearly slipped from Asey's fingers.

"Miss *Curran?* The one that lives in the gray salt-box house on the inlet road? But what in time would she have to do with—" he paused and told himself to slow down. "You mean the one that has all that beachplum jelly out in front? *That* Miss Curran?"

"Not *real* beachplum!" Mildred said. "My mother says it's a gyp!"

"An' I wonder," Asey said, "if this is a *real* plum puddin'—huh! Who'd Miss Curran make it for, someone who was comin' to the cake sale, I s'pose?"

"It had Ann Tinsbury's name on it," Mildred said. "I saw it. Only on account of her being murdered," she added quite matter of factly, "I guess she didn't ever get to buy it."

"I guess as much. You know, this puddin' looks sort of like a Pruneface," Asey held it up in front of headlights again. "Is that how you guessed that Pruneface made it, huh?"

"Oh, *no!*" Mildred giggled. "No, I *saw* it there! Saturday night. It was in her back pantry window, cooling off. I thought it might be a cake, so I went over and looked at it. You see, I was delivering papers for Freddie—he's the blue-star boy for the *Times,* you know. Perhaps you don't know, but that's a pretty important thing to *be*—he gets a free trip all the way to Boston during Christmas vacation! Only he can't ever miss a single night, ever, or he loses it. And he wanted to go to the football game in Harwich Saturday!"

"So you took over, huh?"

"Oh, I often do," Mildred said. "I guess I know that route as well as he does. I know all the people on it. They always talk with me. Except old Pruneface! I never even let her *see* me!"

I see!" Asey said. "I see!"

He thought suddenly of something Lois had said, something about how she and Ann had gone to Miss Curran's house to use the phone, and how Miss Curran had stood menacingly in the doorway and refused even to let them step a foot inside.

That had been a few mornings ago, Lois said.

Saturday morning, perhaps?

Why not? After all, Saturday was baking day!

"I bet," he said, "that she was in the process of makin' this puddin' when the girls come. An' that's why they got such a brush-off that it scared Lois—but why in time would she put this puddin' *here,* of all the places available in the wide world?"

Until Mildred answered him seriously and promptly, Asey didn't realize that he had been speaking his thoughts aloud.

"She wanted to spoil things for Freddie and me, of course! She's *mean!* She *likes* to spoil things! Everybody at school *hated* her when she took Miss Benton's place that time she was sick. She's always spoiling everything! And she," Mildred said ominously, "she better *wait!*"

"On the other hand," Asey said, "why not! What's a better place to rid yourself of somethin' you don't want around than an abandoned mailbox that nobody ever goes to? Why *not* here?"

"It isn't like a *frog!*" Mildred said. "It isn't *funny!*"

"It don't sound to me as if Miss Curran had a lot of sense of humor," Asey said. "Well, let's get on, Mildred. I got to find out what connection there was between her an'—" he broke off. "Hop in! Don't look so dejected! I bet you can find another place. Matter of fact, as long as Freddie doesn't know someone found out about it—"

"*I* do!"

"Wa-el, of course, I know too. But I shan't tell. An' I bet Pruneface never leaves another puddin' here. So whyn't you just pretend everythin's like it was before?" Asey said. "Just stop an' think how awful hard it'll be to find anythin' half as good. Or as squeaky!"

By the time he dropped Mildred off at her home on Mill Road, she was beginning to concede that there was a faint possibility that the old box might not be entirely spoiled, after all.

"Wait, now!" she said as she jumped out of the jeep. "Wait, now, Mr. Mayo—I got to get the cards!"

"Cards?" Asey's mind was too firmly fixed on the pudding to grasp at once what she was talking about. "What cards?"

"Why, the hurricane postcards! The thirty-one packets of hurricane postcards! You bought 'em!" Mildred said. "Don't you *remember*? Outside of the movies, just before you left?"

"Oh, those! Sure!" Asey laughed. "You bring 'em to my house tomorrow—"

"I guess you better wait!" Mildred said. "You might forget again. That'll be seven dollars and seventy-five cents. I figured it out."

"Okay, but I might as well break it to you that five dollars is all I happen to have left on me," Asey said. "Will you take it as a down payment, an' trust me for the rest?"

"I'd trust you *any*wheres!" Mildred said simply. "I'm going to tell mother that all those things she told me about taking rides from —uh—well, just you wait till I get 'em!"

Five minutes later, richer by thirty-one packs of hurricane postcards, Asey and Junior departed, while Mildred squealed goodbyes at them.

Between his desire to find Hanson in a hurry, and send him packing back to the Peeling ménage, and his yearning to drop in on Miss Curran, of the dubious beachplum Currans, Asey felt definitely torn.

He also felt definitely confused.

At least, he thought to himself, there *had* been a square plum pudding. He had proof of it beside him on the seat.

And while he had implicit faith in Mildred's veracity in general, he had to admit that he didn't know whether to accept in their entirety all the tidbits she'd contributed to the pudding problem.

He certainly never would have accepted them from any adult!

If Maggie Peeling, for example, had claimed to have noticed the pudding while substituting for a blue-star paper boy named Freddie, he would have told her to hold her tongue and hide her head. He simply wouldn't have listened to her!

No matter how much he thought around it, there was only one answer to this pudding business. He'd thought so from the first.

But it was utterly fantastic to consider that there could be any connection between Miss Curran, and Ann Tinsbury! The only thing those two had in common was living in the same part of town!

Asey pushed his foot down on the accelerator as he passed by Dr. Cummings' house, where Horner was living, and then he braked quickly, and backed up.

There were lights on in the office, and Hanson's car was parked out in front.

"Huh!" he said. "Well, I can't help it, I got to go in an' see him—an' I bet I get told off by Cummings later, for ignorin' his deputy's orders!"

A moment later, he was simultaneously knocking on the office door, and pushing it open.

"Dr. Horner," he said, "I'm sorry that a series of unforeseen circumstances over which I had no control have forced me to disregard your professional advice about goin' to bed, which otherwise I'd have taken very much to heart. Hanson, I want you to rip over to Maggie Peeling's—it's the old Martin house that used to be East's. Know it? I—for Pete's sakes, what happened to your hand? That Zanies' work?"

"Yes. Your pal," Hanson said. "I just reached down to pat him—more fool I! I didn't pay any attention to it and went and got me a room at Mrs. Fredley's, but I couldn't get to sleep, this stung so. So I got dressed again and came over here—what's been going on, anyway?"

Asey told him.

"So," he concluded, "I want you to go over an' harry them three, if you think you can take it."

"Listen, if you can still get around after that wallop, I guess *I* can!" Hanson said. "Anyway, I napped for a few minutes. Hey, I found out what Steward didn't want his wife to talk about. It's why he always hated Ann Tinsbury so. It's about their daughter. Seems she was killed in an auto accident, years ago. Ann had ordered the chauffeur to drive fast, and he did."

"Huh! An' Steward finally broke down an' told you about it?"

Hanson shook his head. "No. Mrs. Steward did. And if you ask me, she hated Ann even more than he did. I thought we were pretty much set with those two, and now you go digging these other people up—gee, thanks, Horner. I feel a lot better!"

"P'raps," Asey said suddenly, "you'd be willin' to take a look at my wounds, now I'm here?"

Horner and Hanson both whistled appreciatively at the scratches on his neck and shoulders.

"So that," Horner said, "is why you seemed to be so edgy and twitchy—yes, and you tried to tell me, I remember now, and I wouldn't listen. Here, sit down!"

He pushed Asey into the swivel chair in front of Cummings' littered desk.

"Actually," Horner went on, "I never really thought you'd stay in and go to bed like a nice boy. I just said you should, because I felt sure uncle would have told you to, and I knew he'd fuss at me if it ever came out that I hadn't—what're you laughing at?"

"Ouch!" Asey said as alcohol bit into the scratches. "I *was* laughin' at that old photograph of me an' doc an' his first car. Ever notice it, Hanson? By the humidor here on the desk. He drove the car all by himself all the way to Bradbury's—"

"That's the old yellow house with the cupola, huh?" Hanson asked interestedly as he leaned down and peered at the snapshot. "Judge Bradbury's place?"

"Uh-huh," Asey said. "Ouch, that stings! The doc was burstin' with pride at his first drivin', an' his first car, an' everything went wonderful till we got as far as Bradbury's. Then the road narrowed down—it always was kind of a tight squeeze even for a buggy—with all those great trees loomin' on either side. The doc got cold feet."

"Did he quit?" Horner asked.

"He pretended not to, of course. Made his wife get out an' take pictures, an' stalled around. Finally he said sort of sheepish he guessed *I* could drive from there. His wife an' I always kidded him about it, an' she give him that framed photograph, kind of to commemorate it all. Sittin' on the other side of the desk as I usually do, I never noticed that he still had it. I can still get a rise out of him by askin' if some road's wide—hey, that stings!"

"Why not?" Horner said. "It's supposed to. Those big trees went down in the hurricane, Asey, by the way. That's where I got stuck today, and had to walk. Right in front of that cupola job. Remember I told you, Hanson, about my wanderings around the woods? My God," he added, "not your ankles, too? Well, I suppose I should feel fortunate that I've got only one scar from that beast to carry through life!"

Asey chuckled.

"It don't seem to make no difference in the ultimate results whether you get scratched because you pounce at Zanies, or because Zanies loves you dearly! Hanson, will you hop along to Maggie Peeling's for me, then? I got one little job I want to try to look into, an' then I'll join you over there."

"Just six or eight more suspects to unearth, I suppose?" Horner inquired as Hanson left.

"Nope, just one slightly dour lady. An' I don't think she's goin' to relish a midnight caller," Asey said. "She don't even like bein' talked to in broad daylight, much. All set, doc? I feel considerably better. Thanks."

Horner accompanied him to the door.

"Have fun," he said. "And when uncle asks, as he surely will, you can honestly tell him that I advised bed, can't you—oh, you know I don't really care, Asey! After seeing those scratches, I understand. You're all right. I just want the record kept clear for uncle. So long. Oh," he called after Asey, "avoid cats!"

Asey climbed into Junior and started off in the direction of the Curran house.

Just beyond the traffic lights at the four corners in the center of the town, he heard the sharp report of a puncture, and saw the car coming toward him pull over to the side of the road.

He probably would have sailed by without more than a perfunctory feeling of regret, if he hadn't noticed that the car was a black and white checked city taxi.

And if he hadn't caught a glimpse of the rotund passenger who joined the driver in a survey of the damaged tire.

Junior was stopped so hard that he almost stood up on his hind legs.

"Cummings!" Asey said. "Doc!"

"I'm practically not speaking to you," Cummings said. "I'm practically not speaking to anyone at this point—here, you—what's-your-name! Here's your money. Fifty dollars. For your own sake, I hope that vehicle lives long enough to bear you back to Boston. Here's another ten."

"Thanks, doc," the driver said. "How do I get back?"

"Same way you came. Only," Cummings said, "don't hit that hurricane oak in Barnstable, going back. And remember the detour you didn't take before was to avoid that creek! Good night! And what, may I ask," he turned to Asey, "is that thing you're sitting in? You look like something perched on the top of a toad-stool!"

"Doc, where'd you come from?"

"New York. I took a plane to Boston, and that thing there, that taxi, from the airport. Now, Asey, let me tell you—"

"Where's your wife?"

"In New York. I left her a note," Cummings said. "She wasn't around when I heard about this on the radio. Now, I want to tell you just why I'm not speaking to you! I sit here, month in, month out, on this silly stupid sandspit, no excitement, no stimulation, not even the fun of submarine scares or spy scares any more—"

"Nothin'," Asey said, "but a little hurricane!"

"And you're presumably sitting around hammering out tanks, or whatever you do—*I* don't know, you never told me!—and apparently never coming home again. And I hate my patients' silly faces, and they hate mine. They want a new doctor, I want a change. Out of the blue, Jack drops in. That's my chance. All right, I take it! And what happens? The minute my back is turned, you come home, and hell breaks loose—how's the fellow doing?"

"Horner? Fine. He—"

"And listen, Asey, he mustn't know I came back! He's a bright boy, and I'm proud of him, and he mustn't think I didn't have enough faith in him to manage this. I do! The point I want to make," Cummings said, "is that I think it's damned unfair of you to let all this happen the only time I leave this fool, idiot village in God knows how many years—say, where'd you get this thing?" he added as Asey started up the jeep.

"Junior, you mean? I brought Junior home as a present for Jennie," Asey said. "And that reminds me, I haven't remembered yet to tell her it's hers."

"Not bad, is it?" Cummings said. "Heaven compared to that damned taxi! Well, tell me everything, don't stall any longer! In a nutshell, who did it?"

"You think," Asey said, "that I can sum this up in any nutshell in the three or four minutes between here and Miss Curran's house?"

"You can," Cummings said, "if you get to it! Go on!"

Five minutes later Asey said, "Well, that's the gist of it. What do *you* think?"

"Now this is very interesting, by George!" Cummings said. "Stop while I get my cigar lighted, will you? Why, you're lousy with suspects, Asey! Steward hates the girl, he gets her money and King Tinsbury's besides, he's already apparently done some filching from her estate, he was around the woods, that buoy of yours could have come from King's collection—yes, yes, I know all about that collection! Every little boy in town went around for weeks with stolen lobster pot buoys in their hip pockets! Hm. Of course, the same things all go for Steward's wife, too, don't they? She's equally involved!"

Asey nodded.

"Uh-huh, she is. Only it's been sort of tacitly agreed, why I wouldn't know, that she never left the house this afternoon."

"But she could have. And she has a Siamese," Cummings said.

"Hm! Oh, stop the engine and wait a moment, and let me get things straight! You can't be in such a thundering hurry to see Ada Curran—what in the world do you want from her, anyway? Beach-plum jelly? Hers is merely a sin committed under that name. Yes, I always mistrust people with Siamese, Asey. Persians are bad enough, but Siamese!"

"Zanies liked me fine, doc," Asey said. " 'Course, I got clawed up a bit—"

"I said people *with* Siamese, not people Siamese liked! Hm! And Maggie Peeling! Well, I knew Maggie's husband, and I understand her a bit. They came here on their honeymoon—oh, I don't know how many years ago it was, she was about eighteen. Ralph Peeling was probably one of the most unmitigated blackguards I ever ran into," Cummings said. "I don't know whether she finally divorced him, or whether he merely succumbed to the D.T.'s. But Maggie's life with him was no bed of roses. And personally, I wouldn't say that she had the conscience of a small fruit fly. The Tinsbury family's all refusing to help her any with that prospective book on King makes a dandy motive, doesn't it? Maggie's sore they won't help, Maggie threatens Ann a bit, Ann calls her bluff—that's good!"

"I s'pose she could have picked up my buoy on the shore," Asey said. "I'm sure it was her who reeled up the cod line after layin' it out for her bound markin's. I'm sure she saw Ann this afternoon!"

"Oh, I like the sound of Maggie," Cummings said, "even though the Tinsbury money is obviously the best incentive anyone could have for killing the girl. But Maggie was there, Maggie had access to a buoy, and she certainly did her best to cover things up, too!"

"You know this Brian Lemoyne, doc?"

Cummings nodded. "Yes, he's been into the office once or twice. Poison ivy and heat rash, as I remember. I wouldn't know what to say about him, Asey. I wouldn't ever feel sure of the fellow, I think. He's one of those men who finds civilian readjustment a lot tougher than army life. I don't mean to insinuate he's a psycho-neurotic. He isn't. He's also in fine physical health. But he just hasn't found himself yet. Hm. I suppose after you've loved a girl as long as he loved Ann, you finally either sensibly give up, or else you blow up. In his unsettled state, I wouldn't guess which he might do. He said he'd seen Ann this afternoon, did he?"

"Apparently," Asey said, "en route to helpin' an old lady with a hurricaned chicken coop, or somethin' equally good an' noble."

"I sometimes worry about the nobility streak in men like Brian," Cummings said. "They feel they must somehow continue to rise and be heroes. Hm. Then there's Lois Cook—well, of course, she's always been fighting Maggie, all her life, I gathered."

"Know her too?"

"A slight touch of dysentery brought us together," Cummings said. "I'd say the girl had never known what you might call security —she was brought up by Maggie, and with that rotter Peeling in the offing. You never can tell what a young girl like Lois will do in the throes of unrequited love. All of 'em seem to have been there on the scene, don't they—*what* are you starting up for? I'm not nearly straightened out about all this!"

"I told you," Asey said with a chuckle, "I'm callin' on Miss Curran, an' right glad of your company on the job—oh, for Pete's sakes, I never got to tell you about the square plum puddin', did I? Well, I'll catch you up on that!"

"I'm speechless!" Cummings said when he got through. "Literally speechless! Why? That's all *I* can say, *why*? Why'd she make it? Why'd she take it to the sale? Why'd she steal it? Why —in the name of all that's holy, *why* did she stuff it into an abandoned mailbox?"

"Wa-el," Asey said, "there's only one answer. I sort of thought so from the very first."

"Can you bear to enlighten me?" Cummings said. "I mean, mine is a common or garden brain, standard size. It barely comprehends a square plum pudding. It can't make any deductions from it."

"It's my guess," Asey said, "that in with the plum is a good dose of arsenic, or roach powder, or the like."

"Oh, stop!" Cummings said. "Stop! Tell me just one reason **why**

Ada Curran should murder Ann Tinsbury, with square puddings or any other means! Just one reason!"

"Search me!" Asey said. "That's the flaw. Only thing I can think of they had in common is livin' in the same part of town—oh, doc, I'm a dope! Of course!"

"You're obviously misguided in some strange way," Cummings said, "but I doubt if you're really a dope. Of course what?"

"Look, Ann planned to sell her land, didn't she?"

"Did she?"

"Yes, it must be somethin' else I forgot to mention," Asey said. "To some development company."

"Well, what of it? What's that got to do with Ada Curran?"

"Look, doc, development company! That tract'd get all cut up—an' built on—"

"I get it! And the lovely view would go, and Ada's boarding and jelly trade would get shot! Oh, and better than that, Asey, it would shoot the boat works. Her brother's, you know. That shore along there would get all chopped up, and his channel loused up—yes, by George, I think you've got something! Let's go see! Ada's a morbid soul—wait, Asey!"

"What's the matter?"

"You haven't a shred of evidence, you know! Not a shred of proof!"

Asey laughed and started Junior. "I got the puddin'," he said. "Who wants proof? But it occurs to me we also ought to create an unfavorable impression. Let's us be morbid. After all, I don't think she'll be expectin' to have this puddin' trundle back to her so soon, if ever, an' let's us take advantage of it!"

Miss Curran was not in bed, as Asey had fully expected she would be, but sitting at her kitchen table. Account books were spread out before her, and she seemed to be busily figuring.

Asey and Cummings watched her briefly through the glass top of the back door, and then Asey knocked.

She tried to bar the doorway, but Asey strode in past her, and Cummings closed the door and stood in front of it.

"What—" Miss Curran began.

Then, as she watched Asey put the square pudding on the kitchen table, her jaws began to drop.

There was no need to play the scene Asey and Cummings had rehearsed.

Miss Curran broke without it.

Almost before they realized what was happening, she was down on the floor, gripping Asey's knees, crying wildly, sobbing out incoherent words, and demanding forgiveness.

It took ten minutes to put her story together.

She and her brother had wanted to buy a piece of land from Ann Tinsbury, after King died, but Ann had no desire to sell the place except as a whole, and paid no attention to the Curran family's offers. With the breaking up of the Tinsbury land into small lots, the Currans had foreseen an end to their streak of prosperity, if not downright disaster. Their view would be lost, along with the peace and quiet for which Miss Curran's boarders paid so royally. The channel would be bridged, the boat business would go.

"So," Asey said, "you got to broodin' about it, an' decided to kill Ann, huh? An' you made the puddin'—what was in it, arsenic?"

Miss Curran nodded.

"An'," Asey said, "you managed to get it over to the sale without anyone's knowin' who'd brought it. I s'pose if you'd seen on the list that Ann Tinsbury wanted an orange layer cake, you'd have stuffed an orange layer cake with arsenic, too!"

"Wonderful opportunity," Cummings said. "Never thought before of the marvelous possibilities of a to-order cake sale! What got into you to swipe the pudding, Ada?"

"I met Asey, and he talked about Ann—he said she was dead! And I was at the sale and knew she hadn't come! When I got home, I phoned—"

"So it was workin' all the time, was it?" Asey asked.

"I said it wasn't, because I didn't want you around! How was I to know that *you'd* come home?" she said. "I never counted on your being here! And then you appeared there on the beach road!

I didn't know what to think when you said you wanted to phone!" she paused to wipe her eyes. "First I thought you knew about me and the pudding! I thought you'd already found out! I was shaking like a leaf!"

"Ah, conscience!" Cummings said.

"Funny part of it is that she *was*," Asey said. "An' I just thought it was my lookin' like a tramp that scared her! So you phoned—then what?"

"I found Ann hadn't come and got the pudding, after I left the sale. Then I knew it wasn't me who'd killed her, but someone else—"

"An' somehow you thought it out enough to know that the puddin' hadn't better be left around loose, under the circumstances," Asey said.

"Why, it was dangerous! Why, it could have killed someone!" Miss Curran returned.

"I've heard everything!" Cummings said. "By George, now I've heard everything— Asey, did you *hear* what she just said?"

"Uh-huh, I heard. So you decided you'd go an' steal it back, an'," Asey said, "you nearly got caught red-handed in my shed, too! Now, why—"

"For God's sakes, get to that!" Cummings said. "I've been in suspense long enough! *Why* did you put it in the mailbox, Ada?"

Miss Curran said very plaintively that wherever she went, someone was there.

"I couldn't seem to get rid of it! And I didn't want to throw it just anywhere, where some poor animal might eat it, and die!"

"I'm touched," Asey said, "but I'm not awful convinced about them poor animals! I understand what she run into, though, doc. Remember Jennie an' the rubber girdle she couldn't get rid of? Well, so you finally stuck the puddin' in the mailbox. Did you have any intention of doin' anything more about it?"

Obviously, that was as far as Miss Curran had been able to think out. To her, the abandoned letter box was the end.

"Hm. Out of your life forever!" Cummings said. "It's very interesting. These borderline cases, I mean," he added thoughtfully. "A person may live a seemingly normal life, and then he or she gets an obsession, and then—bang! Well, so much for the pudding. That you didn't kill her is obviously no fault of yours! Was your brother in on this, too? Where's Charley?"

"Oh, no, no! He's away, in Maine!" Miss Curran sounded shocked. "*He* didn't know anything about my plan! He'd never have let me, never! I never would have dared if he'd been home!"

"So he," Cummings said, "is the steadying influence, is he? And without him, you run slightly amok. I see!"

"Where's your boarder, Miss Curran?" Asey asked. "Is he home?"

"Mr. Prunn? Oh, yes, he's in bed. He went to bed long ago."

"I want to see him," Asey said. "What room is he in?"

"But *he* didn't know about the pudding, he didn't have anything to do—"

"I know. I just want to see him. Show me where he is."

Asey looked with interest at Armand Prunn when he opened the door of the upstairs bedroom in response to Miss Curran's knock.

Certainly the fellow was the right height, he thought. The right build, too. Blond—but that meant nothing. Brian's normally light-brown hair had been made to appear dark without much trouble!

"Yes?"

"Mr. Prunn," Asey said, "I'm sorry to trouble you. I know that you knew Ann Tinsbury—"

"I have heard of her death. I am very, very sorry." There was just the faintest trace of an accent in his speech. "I do not understand how this has happened to her—will the gentlemen come in? You are perhaps the police, yes?"

"In a manner of speakin'," Asey said, "yes."

He looked at the full ash trays, the evening paper crumpled up on the floor, the magazines on the bed table, the novel lying half open on the bureau. To all outward appearances, Mr. Prunn had been spending a quiet evening, just curled up with some good reading, in Miss Curran's front bedroom.

"I only wondered," he went on, "if you'd happened to have seen Ann Tinsbury today?"

"But yes, this very morning! I am what you may call a suitor," Armand Prunn said, "in a small way. I ask her once more if she will marry me, perhaps, and she says, as always, no. Do sit down, gentlemen!"

He waved hospitably toward a couple of stiff-backed rockers, and proffered cigarettes.

"Do I gather," Asey said, "that you weren't particularly desolated by bein' turned down?"

Armand shrugged as he sat down on the edge of the bed and crossed his legs.

"I am always hopeful," he said. "Always. For the last few years it has been very necessary that I am always hopeful."

"I see," Asey said. "An' Ann didn't seem to be worried about anythin', or anybody?"

"She was, as always, in the best of health and spirits. Me, I cannot comprehend who would do this thing to her. Nor," Armand said, "do I believe it will have occurred to Ann that such a horrible thing could happen to her."

Steward, Asey remembered, had said almost the same thing.

"Thank you, Mr. Prunn." Asey got up from the rocker. "Sorry to have bothered you."

"You mean," Armand's face wore a disconcerted expression, "that is all you gentlemen wish of me?"

"Yes," Asey said, "unless you have anythin' you'd particularly like to tell us. You seem sort of surprised," he added.

Armand's white teeth flashed in a smile. "In my country, gentlemen," he said, "the methods of the police have been quite different. Yes."

As he climbed back into Junior, Cummings finally permitted himself a snort of irritation.

"Didn't work out very well, did it?" he said. "No soap on **Ada** Curran, no soap on the count!"

"I don't know why you say that," Asey returned. "Miss Curran give us a lovely explanation of how she put arsenic in a puddin', an' how she didn't poison Ann Tinsbury. But there's not any particular reason, doc, why she couldn't have killed her just the same, you know!"

"What?"

"Wa-el, is there? She lives near the inlet woods, she could have picked up a buoy, an' she had a motive. No reason why she couldn't have left the puddin' at my house, come back here an' killed Ann, an' so forth an' so on! In short, provin' you didn't kill someone one way don't necessarily prove you couldn't've killed 'em another!"

"Well," Cummings said, "well. Well, I concede the point. Her mind is just borderline enough, just twisty enough to do something like that—all right, I'll concede the point freely. She did spill over and emote pretty quickly! But you drew a blank on the count, didn't you?"

"Oh, no, doc!" Asey said as he started the car. "No, indeed! He's my looter."

Cummings' yelp of disbelief rose over the sound of Junior's engine.

"He is? How'd you know? Whyn't you do something about it? Where are you going? If he's your looter, you crazy nut, what are you going *away* for?"

"I want to think," Asey said, "an' I want to get out of the range of Armand's windows. I got a problem. Sure, I guessed that he was my man, first glance I had of him. An' when I saw the iodine bottle out, an' when he crossed his legs, I knew he was."

"Are you *crazy*? What," Cummings demanded, "what are you talking about?"

"Cat scratches."

"Cat scratches?"

"Uh-huh. On his ankles," Asey said. "Zanies had been after him, too, an' recent. Now," he drew up by the side of the road, "let's figure my problem out. Where do you put your loot? You don't take it away, because no one's seen any trucks. Therefore it's here. Somewhere. Now, I want somethin' unused, an' barny, an' big. Something no one goes to. I want an abandoned mailbox, on a much larger scale. Let's see!"

He started Junior up suddenly, and, ignoring Cummings' protests about speed, drove rapidly to the opposite side of town.

Cummings whistled as he pulled up in front of a large, barnlike edifice.

"Asey!"

"Wa-el, why not, doc? Anythin' more like an abandoned mailbox on a large scale than a summer barn theater? I bet I'm right!"

He forced a window and went in.

Cummings, muttering under his breath about the legality of the situation, followed.

"There!" Asey played a flashlight around. "Antiques, books, an' all the rest. There, that's a load off my mind! Now, we'll go back an' see Armand. I use the term 'we' kind of loose. *You'll* go back an' see him. You'll ask him hurried an' polite if he'll come downstairs, please, there's someone you want him to identify. I'll do the rest."

"Going to jump him?"

"I've learned to take no chances on Prince Torso," Asey said. "This trip, I'm goin' to be waitin' with Miss Curran's clothesline!"

Fifteen minutes later, Cummings gave it as his opinion that Miss Curran's clothesline was very efficient stuff.

"You have before you now only the problem of making him talk," he added. "Something in his face makes me think that nastier men than we have failed in the process."

"We can always try bein' polite," Asey said. "Mr. Prunn, just why have you gone in for this lootin'?"

Armand looked up at him.

"Man must live," he said simply. "And you people in this country are so very, very careless with your possessions!"

Fifteen minutes later, Cummings sighed.

"Well, that's his sentence," he said, "and he's certainly sticking to it! Man must live, and we're so damned careless! Fingerprints'll get him, won't they? Why not turn him over to Hanson?"

"I'm going to. We got him on the lootin' angle," Asey said. "What I wanted was more of the murder angle. Wa-el, even if he won't fill in the chinks, I think I know 'em. He was the lad who jumped me by the bridge, an' the one I mixed with at Tinsbury's. He was there in the inlet woods, too. An' no matter how casual he likes to seem, he'd just got turned down by Ann for the umptieth time. An' she was leavin'. Tie him up in some of your surgical knots, doc, an' we'll stick him in back. Hanson'll þe over at Maggie Peeling's."

Cummings started to laugh as they bundled Armand into the back of the jeep.

"Names," he said in response to Asey's query. "Armand Prunn —think of it by sound! Almond Prune! And—Lemoyne! And Cook! And Peeling. Curran. Steward. Tinsbury! And a square pudding! It just all strikes me as being funny, that's all. The cookery department."

"Mildred's last name," Asey observed, "is Rayson."

"All we need," Cummings said, "is a dash of cinnamon—think he's secure?"

"He should be. We'll stop and pick up Sam at the Tinsbury house. They don't need him any more, their jewels are safe enough now. He can stand guard."

"What in blazes," Cummings said, "have you got on this front seat, anyway? First I sit on that damned pudding, now I sit on packets! What are all these things?"

"Hurricane postcards. Didn't you ever get sold any?"

"Oh, yes, they've been around the house, but I saw enough of the real thing. I don't need to look at pictures. What about things, Asey?"

Asey shrugged.

"Let's see what Hanson's pried out of that lot at Maggie's, first," he said.

Hanson came running out in the driveway to meet them.

"A couple minutes more," he said, "and I'd have gone bats—hey, what you doing here, Sam? What goes on?"

"Your looter," Asey said. "Snap on that outside light an' meet him face to face."

Hanson turned on the light, and then leaned over and peered at Armand.

"So he's the one who walloped you?" he said. "This—hey! Hey, doc! Doc!"

"Nice of you to notice me," Cummings said. "I'm flattered. I want you to know that I've been of enormous assistance. At one point, I held a flashlight while Asey inspected this fellow's loot over in the summer theater. I also lured him out of his bedroom. And for a brief period, I looked menacingly at Ada Curran. You couldn't possibly get on without me—only don't tell my nephew so!"

"The stuff's in the *theater?*"

"Uh-huh," Asey said. "It is. An' I've warned Sam not to undo this lad till you get him in a cell. You'll have to set Jameson on him —he's not talkin'. He's a product of concentration camps an' unrest," he added, "an' he thinks us Americans are very careless folks to leave our things about loose. He's all yours! Put him in Hanson's car, Sam. What did you find out?"

"I think I got it all out of 'em, but at what cost to me!" Hanson said. "Lois says yes, she met Ann, but Ann was in a hurry to get to the post office and they only talked a minute or two. She didn't expect to see Lois again, on account of expecting to be busy with the Stewards after she came back from the sale. She advised Lois to tell Brian what she felt about him. Said she wouldn't be any worse off."

"Sounds reasonable," Asey said.

"Well, maybe. She says that's all that happened between 'em. Maggie's admitted laying the cod line to mark a boundary—that was like pulling teeth! She says on walking the length of it back from the shore, she found Ann's body, and ran like hell. Because only a few minutes before, when she was laying it down, she saw Ann, and spoke to her. She says Ann said she was sorry for the fuss they'd had, but she thought Maggie's talents would show better in a book about someone else, and Maggie says they shook hands—a likely story, if you ask me!"

"Ann was apparently in a benevolent sort of goin' away mood," Asey said. "She turned down your looter nice an' soft in the mornin', we learned, too. What about the reelin' in of that line?"

"She ran away first," Hanson said. "Scared stiff, see? Then she realized she mustn't leave the line there, so she went back and started to reel it in. There was something on the end, and she got scared again and peeked, and saw you—must have been you, I guess! Only she thought it was the murderer. Then you went running off, and she wound up the rest of the line, with that plate on the end, and went home like crazy. You know the rest. She stuck the plate back, and got some new line."

"Huh. How'd you make out with Brian?"

Hanson sighed. "He was the hardest. He claims, Asey, that Ann yelled at him—he was down on the shore helping someone or other rescue a hen coop. Well, Ann yelled at him she was going, and he went up to the path and spoke to her. Said she didn't know when she'd be back, and—"

"Whoa—was this after she'd seen Lois?"

"That's right. And before Maggie, the way I doped it out. None of 'em has any idea about times, of course! Well," Hanson said, "she told him she was a lost cause, and for him to use his head and look at Lois."

"So! Fits in so wonderful, they might almost have planned it! Did Brian explain about stealin' the letters from Tinsbury's?"

"Maggie isn't a girl who gives up easy," Hanson said. "In spite of this chummy talk with Ann, she still wanted those letters to write that book. She whipped up some long-winded story that made Brian think it'd be funny to steal 'em—didn't sound funny to me, I must say! But he claims it was, and he went and snitched the letters. He claims he didn't know about Ann being murdered.

Hadn't heard it on the radio or seen the paper or anything. Say, Asey, how could he have got into Tinsbury's without anyone knowing?"

"Wa-el, *I* did! I s'pose," Asey said, "if we want to be charitable an' give him the benefit of the doubt, we can guess he came while I was listenin' to the Stewards. I didn't hear him. They didn't. If Armand did, while he was stealin' the jewel cases, he didn't mention it—wonder why Brian didn't get scratched, too!"

"Honest, Asey," Hanson said, "I'm dead. I can manage to get this fellow back, but that's about all—what'll we do about the bunch of 'em? One minute I keep thinking they're all guilty as hell, and the next minute, they seem to be innocent little lambs! I feel that way about the Stewards, too!"

"It's also my general impression," Asey said, "about Armand—his name's Armand Prunn, by the way!—an' Miss Curran. Sum her up for him, doc."

Cummings summed her up, in his own picturesque fashion.

"So," Asey said, "you can brood about her, too. An' by the way, Hanson, did you think to ask Brian or Maggie about those lapel pins, an' if she was wearin' two? Well, no matter, we can let it go till tomorrow."

"I'll go ask now," Hanson said. "Jennie reminded me of 'em, but we got sidetracked—"

"Jennie in there?" Cummings interrupted. "I must go see her! Come on in, Asey, you might as well find out about the pins yourself."

Asey shook his head.

"I'm broodin'," he said.

It was, he thought to himself after the pair had disappeared inside, such a silly thing to brood about!

But if Ann Tinsbury had been hurrying to the post office that early in the afternoon, then she was rushing to mail letters, to get them off on the afternoon train. She wasn't going to get letters. The morning mail would have been sorted, the evening mail hadn't come.

"All right!" he said aloud. "Where in blazes *were* her letters she was mailin'? Where are they? Who *took* 'em!"

Without particularly thinking about them, he picked up a packet of the hurricane postcards, broke the string around them, and looked through them.

Those letters had to be somewhere! Someone had taken them!

He stopped suddenly, and looked down at one of the pictures.

He continued to look at it for a long while.

When Cummings and Jennie finally came out with Hanson, he dropped it hurriedly on the seat.

"They both think Ann had on the pins—"

Hanson broke off as another car piled into the driveway, and Horner got out of Cummings' old sedan.

"Couldn't stay away," he said. "Tossed and turned, wondering what you—oh!"

"Look!" Cummings said quickly. "I wasn't ever coming near you, I didn't mean you to know I was back! Truth is, I couldn't stay away from this mess! I'm not going to interfere with you—"

"Look, uncle, if I had another day of this, I'd pop!" Horner said. "I've spent the last hour wondering if I dared write you to come back— I knew I couldn't last one week, let alone two! Truth is, it's more of a pace than I thought! Now, I'm way behind—what's happened?"

"I'll catch you up," Asey said. "Come along in Junior with Jennie an' me—we'll drop you off. Doc can take his sedan back."

"Oh, let me go in Junior!" Cummings said. "I *like* that thing! I've sure taken a fancy to it! I'd give money for one just like it! I—"

"Like Hanson," Asey said, "I have so much stamina, an' no more. We're callin' it a day, an' I'll catch him up on the way back. Come on, Horner. Jennie, sit in back so's I can talk to him."

It seemed to Jennie that there was something definitely wrong with the roads Asey was taking. She started to say so, once or twice, but she couldn't manage to make herself heard.

In the front seat, Asey was talking to Horner.

"So Miss Curran said—hey," he slowed down. "There's the old Bradbury place, the one with the cupola!"

"Oh, yes, this is where I got stuck!" Horner said reminiscently. "They've moved the trees off the road since afternoon, but I had to walk through these woods—"

"Through *these* woods?"

"Why, yes! This is Briar Lane, the place in the photograph. With the cupola!"

Asey leaned back against the car seat.

"Sure, Horner?"

"Why, of course!" Horner sounded amused. "I know, I was stuck right over there! And there's Bradbury's, with the cupola, and I know it's Briar Lane, because it's written on that photograph on uncle's desk. It's right by the inlet woods. I walked from here to old Aunt Mary Swett's."

"All six miles?" Asey asked softly.

"Six? It's only half a mile—"

"It's six. This is the Bradbury house, Horner. It used to be on Briar Lane, an' only half a mile from the inlet woods, an Aunt Mary's. It used to be just where it was in that photograph of Cummings's, on his desk. Only—they moved it, Horner. Ten years ago. It's on Pond Road, now. That's just where you are. Six miles from the inlet!"

"How did you do it?" Horner asked in a strained voice.

"I looked through some hurricane postcards," Asey said. "They been in my pocket, some of 'em, ever since I been home, but I only bothered to look a little while ago. There was one of this place. I remembered, suddenly, that it'd been moved. An' finally, I figured out what you'd done."

"Yes?"

"You weren't *ever* on Briar Lane, but you wanted people to think you *had* been. You *wanted* people to think so, because then, though you would put yourself near the place where Ann was killed, you'd be placing yourself nearer the beginnin' of that path she took!"

"And?" Horner said.

"An' you had a picture right in front of you of a house with a cupola, and Briar Lane written across the front of it. You also had a packet of hurricane postcards, one of 'em was that *same* house with a cupola, an' the road in front of it was all covered with fallen trees. That one didn't *say* Briar Lane. None of them hurricane cards has place names. Only the town name. But you knew—or thought you did. Because it was the same house. You could say you went to the inlet by Briar Lane—not the regular road you actually did take, that put you very near the middle of that path. You could say that you got stuck, an' wandered around, an' walked to your patient. You're a stranger here. It would all make sense."

"And I'd have got away with it, too, wouldn't I?" Horner asked. "If you hadn't come home, and if I hadn't gone too far with a cupola I'd never seen! Okay, Asey. I won't kick and scream. I'll go quietly."

Lois pounced on Asey as he entered his kitchen the next morning.

"Jennie made me wait," she said. "She wouldn't tell me a thing till you came—how did he do it, Asey? What did he do? Why did he do it? How! Tell me!"

"Wa-el," Asey said, "he did it quite easy. He drove out the regular road to the inlet, started walkin' across lots to Aunt Mary's, an' met Ann."

"I didn't know they knew each other!"

"They did! Probably she was the last person he expected to see. He thought she was still abroad. She thought he was in France. An' Ann was a direct person. She said she had just written him a letter. Had it right there. She'd heard casual from someone that he was just openin' a new office in New York. She wanted to know when he'd left the service, an' why had his letters come from abroad if he was home—that was easy enough, he'd fixed it so they would —an' most of all, what about her money?"

"Her money?" Lois said. *"Hers?"*

"Just so. He'd been misusin' money she'd given him for charitable purposes. She accused him of it, an' he killed her. That's the story, in a nutshell."

"But what charitable purposes? What do you mean?"

"You told me yourself about her charitable whims," Asey said. "Horner was one of 'em—though it turned out different than she planned. It all began a year or so ago, when she heard him yearnin' for some money to cure some kid—he was in the navy, an' the affair was beyond his reach. One of those things he couldn't touch, an' none of the outfits of regular relief could, either. Ann forked over the money, the kid got cured. Horner found other cases. Ann supplied the money for them. Horner claims she almost forced it on him."

"Ann would have," Lois said. "He was doing the things she liked best to have done. Her way, too."

"Uh-huh. But it led to the inevitable results," Asey said. "Horner was honest enough at first. But then he kept some money, an' then he kept more. When he got out of the navy, he was in a position to open a swell New York office with fancy equipment!"

"On her money!" Lois said "Oh!"

"Exactly. Ann was no fool. When she heard he was home, an' startin' to practice, she got sore. But, Ann was stuck. She couldn't prove he'd gypped her. The money arrangements was too intricate. All her own fault, too. She insisted on 'em, because she wanted to keep Horner's navy record clear. She didn't want to get him into trouble, she wanted him to keep on with this extracurricular charitable work. But when she met him yesterday, she accused him, quick. Right off the bat. Waved letters at him—one to him, one to her lawyers. Horner had his bag in one hand, an' that buoy of mine in the other—"

"Where'd he get that, anyway?" Jennie asked. "I never did find that out!"

"He'd just stumbled over it in the field, where someone had dropped it—probably started to take it home from the shore, an' then changed their minds. He noticed my name, an' picked it up. Intended to take it back home with him. An' when she accused him, he hit her with it. Then he carried her a distance along the path, an' put her down. He seen Maggie's cod line lyin' there, an' he meant to fix it up so's to look like an accident. Only he didn't have time. He had to leave it over her shoulders, because Maggie was walkin' back along her cod line bound. He had to beat it. But he felt pretty safe."

"He felt fine," Jennie said, "till he got home, an' the phone rang, an' it was *you,* askin' him to come quick! I heard him say that was a body blow!"

"I think it was. That," Asey said, "was when he figured he'd say he went by Briar Lane, instead of the regular road. An' that, you might say, proved his undoin'."

"What about that flower pin, the topaz pin?" Lois asked. "Who took that?"

"It caught in Horner's coat, when he was carryin' her, an' come off. He stuck it in the bottom of his black bag—an'," Asey said, "I'd ought to have had wit enough to have doped that out last night at Tinsbury's house! Zanies was playin' with the bag, an' he pounced on her so quick! But up till then, he'd let *me* handle the cat. I should ought to have guessed he didn't want me near that bag. I'd ought to have caught on sooner, from the way he tried to help me, an' the helpful way he brought up looters. Lots of things should've told me! Like Brian, he hasn't been back long," he added thoughtfully. "He hasn't learned to get used to lots of things, like not hittin' quick—"

He broke off as he saw Cummings walking up the walk to the kitchen. He hadn't seen the doctor since last night, and he almost didn't want to.

"That jeep!" Cummings said offhandedly as he entered the kitchen. "That jeep—hello, Jennie, hello, Lois, hi, Asey! I love that jeep! I'd give a thousand dollars for that jeep!"

"Will you make out the check," Jennie said with equal nonchalance which she also didn't feel, "to the Women's Club?"

"What? Why, sure, if you want! You don't mean—"

"I hate to give it up," Jennie said sadly, "havin' just found out it's mine—but it's a lovely way to rebuild the clubhouse, an' that insurance *was* all my fault. P'r'aps you'll let me drive it some-times—"

"Doc," Asey said, "I'm awfully sorry about him!"

"I know. I knew last night." Cummings paused. "The minute I saw your face when I came out of Maggie Peeling's, I knew. Felt pretty badly about it, but—oh, well. Speaking of names," he went on, "I hope you realize his is Jack Horner—what's that?" he broke off suddenly and pointed under the stove. "That cat! *Not* the Siamese!"

"The Stewards brought him, this morning," Jennie looked at Asey and they both knew the moment they'd been dreading was over. "He was fussin' so, they couldn't take him with 'em. They gave him to Asey. I certainly hope he'll be *happy,* because it's goin' to be a terrible comedown for him, after all that wealth an' luxury—"

"And what," Cummings interrupted, pointing to the kitchen table, "what in God's name is that collection of pies, and cakes, and puddings! *Another* cake sale?"

Asey chuckled.

"Oh," he said, "that's the sort of food you give people when they're sick, or when you feel awful sorry about somethin'. That's the reaction."

"The *what?*"

"Reaction. Everyone thought I was a murderer, last night," Asey said, "but now the reaction's settin' in. Those are gifts to me. An' if you want to know, I'm not goin' to eat one of 'em! I've had all the provin' of puddin's that I want for a lifetime!"

Available from Foul Play Press

The perennially popular Phoebe Atwood Taylor whose droll "Codfish Sherlock," Asey Mayo, and "Shakespeare lookalike," Leonidas Witherall, have been eliciting guffaws from proper Bostonian Brahmins for over half a century.

Asey Mayo Cape Cod Mysteries

The Annulet of Gilt	288 pages	$5.95
The Asey Mayo Trio	256 pages	$5.95
Banbury Bog	176 pages	$5.95
The Cape Cod Mystery	192 pages	$5.95
The Criminal C.O.D.	288 pages	$5.95
The Crimson Patch	240 pages	$5.95
The Deadly Sunshade	297 pages	$5.95
Death Lights a Candle	304 pages	$5.95
Diplomatic Corpse	256 pages	$5.95
Going, Going, Gone	218 pages	$5.95
The Mystery of the Cape Cod Players	272 pages	$5.95
The Mystery of the Cape Cod Tavern	283 pages	$5.95
Octagon House	304 pages	$5.95
Out of Order	280 pages	$5.95
The Perennial Boarder	288 pages	$5.95
Proof of the Pudding	192 pages	$5.95
Sandbar Sinister	296 pages	$5.95
Spring Harrowing	288 pages	$5.95

"Surely, under whichever pseudonym, Mrs. Taylor is the mystery equivalent of Buster Keaton."
—Dilys Winn

Leonidas Witherall Mysteries (by "Alice Tilton")

Beginning with a Bash	284 pages	$5.95
File for Record	287 pages	$5.95
Hollow Chest	284 pages	$5.95
The Left Leg	275 pages	$5.95

Available from bookshops, or by mail from the publisher: The Countryman Press, Box 175, Woodstock, Vermont 05091-0175. Please include $2.50 for shipping your order. Visa or Mastercard orders ($20.00 minimum), call 802-457-1049, 9-5 EST, Monday–Friday.

Prices and availability subject to change.

Now Back in Print

Margot Arnold

The complete adventures of Margot Arnold's beloved pair of peripatetic sleuths, Penny Spring and Sir Toby Glendower:

The Cape Cod Caper	*192 pages*	*$ 4.95*
Death of a Voodoo Doll	*220 pages*	*$ 4.95*
Death on the Dragon'sTongue	*224 pages*	*$ 4.95*
Exit Actors, Dying	*176 pages*	*$ 4.95*
Lament for a Lady Laird	*221 pages*	*$ 4.95*
The Menehune Murders	*272 pages*	*$ 5.95*
Toby's Folly (hardcover)	*256 pages*	*$18.95*
Zadock's Treasure	*192 pages*	*$ 4.95*

"A new Margot Arnold mystery is always a pleasure . . . . She should be better known, particularly since her mysteries are often compared to those of the late Ngaio Marsh."

—*Chicago Sun Times*

Joyce Porter

American readers, having faced several lean years deprived of the company of Chief Inspector Wilfred Dover, will rejoice (so to speak) in the reappearance of "the most idle and avaricious policeman in the United Kingdom (and, possibly, the world)." Here is the series that introduced the bane of Scotland Yard and his hapless assistant, Sgt. MacGregor, to international acclaim.

Dover One	*192 pages*	*$ 4.95*
Dover Two	*222 pages*	*$ 4.95*
Dover Three	*192 pages*	*$ 4.95*
Dover and the Unkindest Cut of All	*188 pages*	*$ 4.95*
Dover Goes to Pott	*192 pages*	*$ 4.95*
Dover Beats the Band (hardcover)	*176 pages*	*$17.95*

"Meet Detective Chief Inspector Wilfred Dover. He's fat, lazy, a scrounger and the worst detective at Scotland Yard. But you will love him."

—*Manchester Evening News*

Available from bookshops, or by mail from the publisher: The Countryman Press, Box 175, Woodstock, Vermont 05091-0175. Please include $2.50 for shipping your order. Visa or Mastercard orders ($20.00 minimum), call 802-457-1049, 9-5 EST, Monday–Friday.

Prices and availability subject to change.